Jake brought out
the worst in her

Leigh clenched her teeth. The strain of being trapped in an elevator with the arrogant Jake St. John was beginning to play on her nerves.

Jake watched her closely, seeing more of her inner self than she realized. "Isome hum now?" he

"One of you coldly.

"What about

"You mean my boyfriends?"

"No, I mean men. You're not a teenager, Leigh. You've been married. I don't imagine a fumbled kiss from some callow youth would satisfy your needs."

"I don't have any needs," Leigh snapped.

"Don't lie," Jake said dangerously. "At least have the decency to tell the truth, Leigh. We all have needs," he said silkily, "and you don't have to deny yours any longer."

ELIZABETH OLDFIELD
is also the author of this

Harlequin Presents

604—DREAM HERO

Many of these titles are available at your local bookseller.

For a free catalog listing all available Harlequin Romances and Harlequin Presents, send your name and address to:

HARLEQUIN READER SERVICE
1440 South Priest Drive, Tempe, AZ 85281
Canadian address: Stratford, Ontario N5A 6W2

ELIZABETH OLDFIELD

second time around

Harlequin Books

TORONTO • NEW YORK • LOS ANGELES • LONDON
AMSTERDAM • PARIS • SYDNEY • HAMBURG
STOCKHOLM • ATHENS • TOKYO • MILAN

Harlequin Presents first edition July 1983
ISBN 0-373-10608-4

Original hardcover edition published in 1982
by Mills & Boon Limited

CHAPTER ONE

IMPERCEPTIBLY the engine note changed and the jumbo
jet began its ponderous descent, falling slowly through
the dark tropical sky. After travelling halfway across
the world it was now over rubber trees—thousands of
green acres where they stood stiffly to attention, row by
row, like an army of well drilled soldiers. Then came
palm oil plantations, the broad branches meeting overhead in gloomy cloistered arches. Finally the plane
reached the island, passing first over its northern coast,
above high-rise apartment blocks and the low rusted
corrugated iron roofs of kampongs. It took a wide arc,
sweeping southwards. Leigh peered forward eagerly.
Through the cabin windows she caught glimpses of
twinkling lights on ships anchored far below in the harbour. Towering skyscrapers jostled for position on the
shoreline. They were the regional bases for international
banking and trading companies which brought wealth
to the island.

Leigh smiled and a warm glow of pleasure crept into
her. It was good to be back. The doubts on the wisdom
of her journey began to fade and the uncertainties which
had tempted her to abandon her plans at Heathrow were
disappearing. She took a deep breath and relaxed.

'First time in the Far East?' asked the big man in the
seat beside her.

'No. I lived here once, for six months.'

'Did you enjoy it?'

'Very much.'

Unexpectedly her wide blue eyes filled with tears, and
she looked quickly away, out into the velvet blackness
of the night. She was surprised at herself. She had considered her emotions were under tighter control, neatly
ordered behind a bland, protective mask. It was many
months since she had wept, but she realised un-

comfortably that she must still be vulnerable. The routine back home which had carried her along automatically, providing security in the predictable pattern of each day, had now been swept aside. By returning to Singapore she was taking the chance of opening old wounds. She must be on her guard, she decided, with a brisk mental shake of her head.

'These long-haul journeys are murder, aren't they?' continued the man cheerfully, in his broad Australian accent, 'Sixteen hours flying is one heck of a stretch, and I'm not finished yet. I have to change planes for Brunei. I work for an oil company there.'

'Out on a rig?' Leigh's face brightened with interest.

'Sometimes on rigs, sometimes on land,' he replied, warming to her attention. What a beaut she was, with those soft, full lips and cascade of shiny auburn hair. She'd go down a treat with the roustabouts— they'd flip over that shapely figure in the neat blue denim trouser suit. He glanced down at the wedding band on her finger. Some man was fortunate to have this lovely girl as his wife.

'Are you going to join your husband?'

'He died almost two years ago.' Her voice was carefully impersonal. 'In Singapore. This is the first time I've been back since then.'

'I'm sorry.'

She gave a small nod, accepting his sympathy, then turned away, remembering how excited she and Patrick had been on their first journey to South-East Asia. They had been married only a few months when he had been offered a transfer to the Singapore headquarters of the company. She remembered how he had met her out of work, grinning broadly, impatient to tell her the good news.

'What an opportunity!' he had beamed, his brown eyes shining as he had clasped her to him in an enthusiastic bear-hug. 'It's a real step up the ladder, and what a salary! If we save hard we'll be able to buy ourselves a stately home when we come back to England.'

But there had been no stately home. Patrick had never

returned to his homeland. His ashes were scattered on the hard red earth of the Orient.

The seat-belt signs flashed on. The huge plane shuddered, there was a puff of burnt rubber, and they were on land again. Leigh collected up her belongings—the airline bag, the bottle of duty-free malt whisky for Frank.

'Singapore's a great little island, isn't it?' commented the Australian as they waited patiently in the queue to disembark.

'I love it,' she said sincerely. 'I love the people—the Chinese, the Malays, the Indians—all living together in harmony, creating a new nation.'

'How do you like the climate?' he asked, as the familiar humid warmth hit them at the top of the steps as they left the aircraft. Leigh's nostrils were filled with the smell of the tropics, a unique mixture of exotic blossoms, strange spices and drains.

'It can be rather hot at times,' she admitted with a grin, 'but there are distinct advantages to having summer twelve months of the year. It was cold and miserable back home, I'm looking forward to soaking up some sunshine.'

Efficiently they were channelled through Immigration, baggage collection and Customs. The Australian insisted on carrying her suitcase as far as the greeters lobby, then he gave a smiling salute of farewell and disappeared into the crowd. Leigh hesitated, lost in a sea of Singaporeans waiting to meet friends and relations. It was odd to see again so many heads of gleaming jet black hair. There was no sign of Bridget's glowing auburn curls or Frank's tousled grey mop amongst the crowds, and she wondered where they were. Bridget had said in her letter that they would be at the airport to meet her. She shrugged. It was obvious Bridget was running true to form—late again! She picked up her suitcase and walked slowly down the length of the vast arrivals hall, scanning the faces. With her free hand she carelessly tossed back a wayward strand of auburn hair, and a tall American, towering head and shoulders above the tiny Asians, pursed his lips, savouring the unconscious grace of the gesture. Everywhere she went men noticed her, admiring the slender body, the long legs, the swing of her hair as she walked. Abruptly she stopped, putting down the heavy suitcase on the tiled floor. Despite the air-conditioning she was beginning to feel warm, but then Singapore is less than a hundred miles from the Equator. She stripped off her jacket to reveal a sleeveless pink top.

'Leigh, my darlin'!' The shout rang out from the far end of the hall, and everyone looked round, startled. A short, bosomy woman in her early fifties was ploughing through the crowds, scattering people in all directions in her haste. As she neared Leigh her arms opened wide, and a delighted grin almost split her face in two. She clasped the girl to her, raining noisy kisses on her cheeks with all the enthusiasm of a Labrador puppy. 'How good it is to see you again, my darlin'!' she cried, her plump face flushed with the exertion of her race through the airport. 'I'm so sorry I'm late. Have you been waiting long? Did you have a smooth flight? Was the plane full?' She paused for breath. Leigh laughed. Bridget had not changed. She had always been a human whirlwind, always arriving at the last minute, always full of questions. Bridget patted her stiffly lacquered hair with a manicured hand. Her long nails were scarlet, and there was a sparkling ring on each finger. Discretion was not a facet of her personality.

'How are you?' she asked, grabbing Leigh's airline bag before she could protest. 'I was delayed at the hairdressers. Come on, come on.' Her faint Irish accent turned the words into a lilting chant. 'Follow me,' she instructed over her shoulder, and trotted energetically away, leaving Leigh to follow on as best she could through the crowds. For a heavy woman Bridget showed remarkable agility, and it was all Leigh could do to keep her in view as she disappeared ahead through automatic sliding glass doors on to the covered porchway where a conglomeration of cars, taxis, pick-up vans and minibuses waited to whisk travellers away to their various destinations. Fortunately her brightly coloured hair and emerald green dress indicated her position in the mêlée, and Leigh joined her, breathing heavily. 'Where's Frank?' she asked, looking around.

'Oh, I forgot to tell you,' Bridget gave a trill of laughter. 'What a scatterbrain I am! He's away in Hong Kong. He comes home tomorrow. He sends his apologies.'

'Work must come first,' Leigh said with a grin. 'I envy him. I'd love to visit Hong Kong.'

'Frank's sick of it. He's been up there so often just lately. He's involved with the financial side of a deal Rory is trying to swing. Remember I told you about Rory in my letters? He's the Chairman's son.'

Leigh nodded.

'It's a multi-million-dollar transaction,' Bridget continued. 'If he pulls it off it will be a real feather in his cap. There's fierce competition from that Dutch firm, de Groots.'

'Isn't Jake involved?' Leigh asked carefully.

'He will be, when the contract has to be signed, but he's deliberately allowed Rory to handle this his own way. After all, Rory is destined to take over the reins from his father, Sir Clive, before too long, so he has to prove his worth.'

'And how is Jake?' Leigh was aware of an illogical catch in her throat.

'Fine.' Bridget gestured wildly as a cream-coloured Mercedes Benz drew up alongside the porch. 'Here's Yacob with the car. Now you sit in the back with me, my darlin'. Yacob will stow your suitcase in the boot.'

The smiling, brown-skinned Malay driver climbed out of the car to deal with Bridget's torrent of instructions. Leigh smiled to herself. Bridget was obviously still organising everyone like crazy. No doubt the absent Frank continued to fall in with her plans. Not that he was downtrodden, Leigh recalled, indeed he often quietly put his wife firmly in her place when he considered she was overstepping the mark. But fundamentally his main concern was having a quiet life, and he allowed the vivacious Bridget to plan and scheme so long as she didn't disrupt his contentment. Evening after evening her chatter would flow heedlessly over his head as he puffed on his pipe, read his book and murmured the occasional noncommittal word in the right places. Their system worked well. Bridget sang his praises loudly, eternally grateful for his good humour, while Frank sailed calmly along, his wife having already smoothed the path he trod.

Yacob closed the lid of the boot and Bridget, her overseeing completed, climbed into the car. 'You look wonderful,' she declared, chunky jade bracelets jangling on her plump wrists as she surveyed the girl beside her. 'Perhaps a little more mature, but that's hardly surprising when you consider the troubles you've been through. Are you over it now?' Her tone dropped to confidentiality.

'I think so. Thank you very much for your invitation. A month in the sun is just what I need, and it's so good to see you again.'

Bridget leaned across and patted her hand. 'It's good to see *you*,' she exclaimed as the car pulled away from the airport buildings, out on to the road which led to the city. 'You and Patrick were always like part of the family. Poor Patrick . . .' Her voice faded away, and for a few minutes she sat in silence.

The car's headlights illuminated flowering bushes on the central reservation—purple allamanda, bright red pagoda flowers, pink hibiscus and creamy mussaenda. Leigh's thoughts retreated. Frank and Bridget O'Brien had welcomed her and Patrick when they had first arrived to live on the island two years ago. Frank was Chief Accountant at the Singapore offices of Milwain International, the company for which Patrick had worked. Milwains were leading manufacturers, worldwide, of earth-moving vehicles. Frank and Bridget had virtually adopted the young couple, introducing them to the social scene, easing them into the expatriate lifestyle. Six months later they had comforted her in the dreadful days after Patrick's death.

'It's been a comfort to receive your letters and know

that you've managed to pick up the threads again.' Bridget's eyes twinkled. 'Any boy-friends around?' Her curiosity was notorious. It always gained the upper hand, though her interest was goodnatured.

'One or two,' Leigh admitted with an amused twitch of her mouth as the older woman sat up straight, her face taking on a look of bright intent. 'But there's no one serious. I've never met anyone special since Patrick died. Never been particularly interested.'

'Don't you worry, my darlin',' Bridget gave a little wink. 'I've arranged one or two outings for you.'

'I didn't come here to embark on a romance,' Leigh exclaimed with a hint of exasperation. 'I hope you haven't compromised some unsuspecting man. I'm perfectly capable of handling my own love life.'

'I'm sure you are, but I want you to have a good holiday, and besides, there are some very attractive young men here.'

'Like Jake?' Leigh's tone was crisp.

'Like Jake,' Bridget confirmed, not noticing the coolness of the query. 'Though he'd be furious if I ever tried to compromise him. He's much too independent.'

Leigh tugged at her bottom lip with her teeth. Her immediate response on receiving the O'Briens' generous invitation had been to accept, but suddenly she felt a stab of uncertainty as she wondered how she would react to meeting Jake again. She looked thoughtfully out of the car window. Would it have been wiser to have booked a European package holiday with a girl friend? Well, it was too late now. She was here, and would doubtless see him some time during the coming month. She settled back against the smooth leather upholstery and decided she was being foolish. After all, she had thrust aside the trauma of Patrick's death and Jake's role in it. She was worrying unnecessarily. Jake would probably want nothing at all to do with her, she thought grimly, recalling their last vitriolic meeting.

'How's your job?' Bridget's voice intruded.

'Hard work,' she gave a mock groan, 'but I love it.

I'm personal assistant to the managing director of a group of companies, so it means long hours and high pressure. My boss is a hyper-active businessman, and I travel all over the United Kingdom with him, visiting the various factories and offices. I'm always rushed off my feet. I have to take notes, minutes of meetings, that kind of thing. I hold the fort when he's away, make his travel arrangements, deal with contracts. It's all top gear stuff.'

And I'm grateful it is, she thought to herself. I only feel properly alive when I'm at work. Evenings and weekends are dull. Since Patrick died I can't discover how to brighten up my life, or perhaps I just don't want to.

'Is he eligible?' Bridget asked eagerly.

For a moment Leigh looked puzzled. 'You mean my boss? Not unless you call a middle-aged man with middle-aged spread, a wife and three children eligible!' she laughed.

'But you have dates?'

'Yes, but I really have no desire to become involved with a man. I'm perfectly happy with things the way they are.'

That's a lie, she thought ruefully. Well, half a lie. It's true I don't want a man around, but I'm not really happy. Life might be safe and secure, but it was rather bland. Perhaps Singapore would provide a welcome change of pace, but then she wondered again at the wisdom of returning to the island state where she and Patrick had been so happy together. She sighed softly, feeling suddenly vulnerable. The long journey was beginning to take its toll, and the nervous energy which had kept her functioning was fading. She had managed to sleep for a few hours on the plane, but it had been a shallow, fitful sleep. She had been continually aware of figures moving up and down the aisle, and the muffled hum of conversation. Trapped in her seat, she had been unable to stretch her legs, or find a comfortable position. Now she was disorientated by the long flight and the time change. She felt prone to doubts.

'Did your boss object to you taking a month's holiday?'

'Not at all. He's flying to the States for six weeks, so there'll be a lull at the office. Besides, I've worked so much overtime he could hardly refuse.'

They passed an ornate Chinese temple, a fiery dragon perched atop its green glazed roof tiles, and Leigh eyed it with interest. The old excitement at being in the East began to seep into her, despite her tiredness.

'Is Frank still Tuan Number Two?' she asked with a grin.

Bridget chuckled, remembering the old joke. One of the office boys had christened Frank 'Tuan Number Two! Tuan being the Malay term for boss. Jake St John was 'Tuan Number One', and Patrick had claimed the title 'Tuan Number Three' for himself.

'Naturally. How could the company survive without Frank knocking out his pipe tobacco all over the carpets! They need someone slow and steady as a foil for Jake. He's still rushing around all over the place. He virtually lives in planes.'

'He's a workaholic,' said Leigh with more bitterness than she intended.

Bridget cast her a sidelong glance. 'He's a good father,' she defended. 'Although he travels widely during the week he has an unbroken rule to spend the weekends at home with Benjy.' Her face softened as she thought of Jake's son. 'He's almost six years old now, and he's a lovely little boy, so well mannered. Mind you, Jake's very strict with him, too much so at times. I keep telling him that Benjy needs a bit of spoiling, a woman's touch. I do wish Jake would marry again and provide him with a proper mother.'

'I dare say it's not your fault he's still unattached,' Leigh commented wryly, a smile lifting the corner of her full mouth. Bridget was well known as a matchmaker. 'No doubt you've paraded sufficient females before him to fill a harem!'

Bridget's eyes shone. 'One or two—hundred,' she confessed.

'He's choosy?'

'Very. He doesn't like me giving him a helping hand as far as women are concerned, but it's five years since his wife died and he shows no inclination to find himself a new one. Not that he's short of girl-friends,' Bridget snorted. 'He's worked his way through the entire range of women out here—European, Thai, Filipino. You should see Choo, his housekeeper. She's beautiful— Chinese, with those gorgeous slanty eyes.' Her voice dropped and she eyed the driver thoughtfully. 'Perhaps it would be wiser to change the subject.' She leant closer to Leigh. 'Yacob doesn't speak much English, but he might catch the gist of what we're saying, and Jake would be livid if he discovered we were gossiping about him.'

Leigh smiled. She wondered if Jake had any inkling that he was a constant topic of Bridget's conversation. He certainly provided her with sufficient material, she thought caustically, remembering the succession of girl-friends in the past. Mind you, it had to be recognised that he was discreet. He was a good-looking man, Leigh admitted to herself, and it was obvious women found him attractive. And although his public behaviour had always been beyond reproach Jake's restrained aura of virile sexuality made Bridget's surmising about his private life seem immensely possible. Leigh was sure the old proverb was true in his case—there was no smoke without fire. 'How are Angela and Ian?' she asked, abandoning Jake with something approaching relief.

Bridget beamed. Her grown-up children were a topic dear to her heart, and she immediately dived into her handbag to produce dog-eared photographs of Angela's two small children, photographs which had been handed round incessantly. Leigh made requisite murmurs of admiration and was regaled with a long and detailed account of their achievements.

'The baby's potty trained already,' Bridget crowed, 'and little Paul can write his name, and he's only three.' Then she switched to Ian, who was amazing everyone with the brilliant reports he received from his professors at Cambridge. Leigh's mind began to wander. She remembered the first time she had arrived in Singapore.

'There's Jake,' Patrick had said as they stood patiently in a long queue at the Customs checkpoint. An ageing hippy had created a bottleneck as he argued heatedly about the liquor he wanted to take into the country, and his abrasive attitude had provoked the Customs official into a painstaking examination of every piece of his luggage, which included a shabby rucksack and several untidily wrapped brown paper parcels. Leigh had followed Patrick's waves and smiles, but was unable to pick anyone out in the distant crowd. She had never met Jake St John, but already felt faintly antagonistic towards him. Patrick had been convinced Jake had been responsible for the offer of a posting abroad. Years ago they had worked together at the company's London headquarters. Patrick had occupied a junior niche, and had been flattered when Jake, already in a position of some authority, had taken an interest in him and his work. He was grateful to the older man for his friendship, but Leigh had been scathing. She felt his admiration bordered on hero-worship.

'I'm sick and tired of hearing about the wonderful Mr St John,' she had snapped one evening when Patrick had been enthusing over the prospect of working alongside Jake again. 'The only reason he wants you to manage the Far Eastern Sales Department is because you're good at your job. All right, so he may have mentioned your name in the right ears, but you landed the promotion through your own ability. Naturally he wants you to devote all your energies to his branch of the business, he knows how reliable and hardworking you are!'

'Calm down!' Patrick had laughed, unruffled. 'You'll like him when you meet him, everyone does. The girls in the office used to go weak-kneed if he so much as glanced their way. I expect he still has the same effect, he's quite a Lothario.'

She had tightened her lips. She hadn't much time for

lady-killers, and Jake St John appeared to fit the description precisely.

The hippy was asked to retire to a private room for further investigation, and the queue moved forward. As they rounded the barrier into the reception area a tall, wide-shouldered man with dark blond hair thrust out his hand to Patrick in greeting.

'Hello there, it's good to see you again.' He smiled broadly, obviously delighted to renew their friendship, his white, even teeth contrasting with the golden tan of his face. Patrick introduced Leigh and she, in turn, was included in the warm greeting and had received a firm, dry handshake and a shrewd glance of approval. Her feelings of tentative hostility had dissolved in the light of his smile. Patrick had been right, she had liked Jake. Initially. Hatred had come later.

Bridget continued chattering in full spate as they drove into the city. The dingy shop houses and suburban homes gave way to sophisticated shopping precincts and hotels. The traffic became heavier; the five-lane carriageway was solid with a variety of vehicles. A long line of trishaws, pedalled by sinewy Chinese, waited at the kerbside to take the evening's collection of tourists on a tour of the night spots.

'Don't you find it lonely, living by yourself in your bungalow?' Bridget asked interestedly.

'It is quiet, but I'm settled there.'

During the first anguished days when she had returned alone to England after Patrick's death she had, at her parents' insistence, lived with them. She had numbly concurred with all their wishes, pulling their love around her like a blanket to protect the raw hurt. At that time she had had no wish to return to the bungalow which she and Patrick had bought as newlyweds. For weeks she had stayed with her parents, weeks which faded into each other, grey and dim, when she was only aware of pain. Eventually time began the healing process, and she felt the need to be independent again. She returned to the bungalow.

'We're nearly home. Wait until you see our new

apartment,' Bridget piped as they turned into a tree-lined cul-de-sac. Yacob parked the Mercedes in its allotted space before a lofty apartment block and retrieved Leigh's luggage. As they walked past swaying palms and sparkling fountains into the vestibule Bridget gave chapter and verse as to why they had chosen this particular location, and the problems she had encountered in furnishing her home. A circular lift whisked them up to the twenty-third floor where Yacob deposited the suitcase and bade them a smiling goodnight.

'How do you like our new abode?' Bridget's bejewelled fingers flashed as she flung her arms wide, encircling the spacious split-level living room with its white marble floor and vivid Persian rugs.

Luxury oozed from every corner.

'It's beautiful,' said Leigh. She had garnered from her hostess's conversation that much time and money had been devoted to the grandisement of the apartment. A combination of Oriental and Western furnishings had created a refined, yet striking, effect. The dining area was located on the upper level of the room, while down three shallow steps was a wide living section, dominated by a vast, semi-circular window which gave spectacular views over the island and the distant sea. A huge off-white sofa in raw silk had been specially designed to accommodate the curved contour, and glossy-leaved plants cascaded from bronze tubs and hanging macramé holders. In the twenty years the O'Briens had lived away from Ireland they had resided in many countries, and the room was filled with their collection of treasures—Korean chests, pale green Thai celadon lamps, polished yellow gongs from Indonesia, carved wooden statues.

'Would you like something to eat? I can easily rustle up an omelette?' Bridget suggested. 'Or perhaps something to drink?' She indicated a brass makan carrier which held a variety of bottles.

'No, thank you,' Leigh groaned. 'There were endless meals on the plane, but I'd like a cup of coffee if that's possible, then I must go to bed. I'm exhausted!' She rubbed her hand wearily across her brow.

'Just settle yourself down, my darlin'. I'll make some instant, it won't take long.' Bridget returned within minutes. She set down a steaming jug on a glass-topped rattan table and poured two cups of coffee.

Leigh took a welcome sip. 'I like the peacock chair.' She nodded in the direction of an extravagant white chair, shaped like a throne, in intricately worked rattan.

'That's Benjy's favourite. He makes a beeline for it whenever he comes. He sits on it with a very hoity-toity expression.'

'Do you see him much?'

'About once a week. I take him to the cinema or the zoo. Choo never takes him out. I suppose she looks after him perfectly adequately, but she's too tied up with that baby of hers to give Benjy any excursions.'

'Choo has a baby?' Leigh raised her eyebrows in surprise.

Bridget's face tightened with displeasure. 'She was pregnant when Jake took her on. She's the daughter of some business associate of his in Jakarta. She came over here for the birth—hospital care is far superior in Singapore. I thought she'd return home after the baby was born, but it has some kind of heart defect. It's been in and out of hospital since it was born.' Bridget's tone was scornfully impatient. 'It was about that time that Jake's aunt, who'd been looking after Benjy, decided to return to England. She was getting too old to cope, poor soul. Choo had been helping out with Benjy, and so she stayed on, as his housekeeper!' Bridget grunted disdainfully. 'It's an arrangement which appears to suit everyone, especially Jake.'

Leigh drank her coffee thoughtfully.

'He seems to have his life well organised.'

'You bet! I don't know what he gets up to with Choo, but it's hard to believe their relationship is purely a working one. She's the prettiest little thing, no man could ever resist her.'

Leigh escaped to the welcome solitude of her room as soon as was politely possible. Bridget's never-ending chatter was beginning to jar on her shattered nerves.

The adrenalin which had supported her through the twenty hours since she had left home back in England had dissipated, and now her eyelids were heavy, and her body weary. All she wanted to do was sleep. She switched off the bedroom air-conditioner and opened wide the window. The apartment was fully enclosed and could be kept at a controlled moderate temperature, but she preferred to feel the natural balmy air of the tropics. For a few moments she gazed out at the city. At night it was a wonderland. White lights glittered on soaring housing blocks, while far below in the streets the lights of vehicles wove a moving pattern of red and gold. An upside-down moon hung in the inky blackness of the sky, a solitary silver observer, watching over the island.

She undressed quickly and slid between the sheets. Her unpacking could wait until the morning. She hadn't brought a nightdress, they were superfluous in the heat. She and Patrick had always slept in the nude. Perhaps it had stimulated their love life, or perhaps it was because they were young and newly married, but they never seemed able to have enough of each other. She smiled wistfully in the darkness. Their lovemaking had been so good. Her body cried out for him, even now. No other man had aroused her since his death. Not that she had given anyone the chance. She had deliberately chosen as friends men who were sexually 'safe', men who would not demand too much. She had always been in control of her relationships, steering them safely away from passionate embraces. She realised some of the men she had dated considered her frigid, noting the way she stiffened and retreated if they ventured to kiss her mouth. She didn't care, she thought defiantly. She didn't want a lover; she only wanted Patrick.

The following day was a lazy one.

'Jet-lag is very tiring. You must take life easy for a while,' Bridget decreed. 'You must give your body clock time to adjust.'

'That's fine by me,' Leigh smiled lethargically. 'All I want to do is lie beside the pool and sunbathe.'

'Do you mind if I don't join you? My skin shrivels

like a prune in the sun, and, to be honest, I get bored doing nothing.'

'Not at all.' Leigh was secretly relieved to have some time on her own. She put on a rainbow-coloured bikini, covered it with a pink towelling robe, and took the lift down to the swimming pool in the gardens of the apartment block. She was perfectly content to lie beside the shimmering water, idly watching fretted fonds of palm trees moving against the forget-me-not blue of the sky. One or two other sun-worshippers were lying around languidly, and she gave them a tepid smile, unwilling to become embroiled in conversation. She found herself a lounger, and lay back. Later she swam a little, read a cheap paperback, stroked on tanning lotion and soaked up the sun, alternating between its burning glare and the shade of a gaily striped umbrella. She was grateful for the time to relax, for she knew that once Bridget deemed her to be in full working order again tranquillity would become a thing of the past.

She and Bridget were sipping a pre-prandial sherry in the early evening when Frank arrived home. After greeting his wife he opened wide his arms and enveloped Leigh in a comfortable hug.

'It's good to see you again, my dear.' He stood back and surveyed her. 'It's not too disturbing, is it, returning again? You're not on some kind of morbid pilgrimage?'

'Certainly not! I wouldn't have come if I didn't consider myself fully recovered,' she lied, remembering the moment on the plane when she had felt the prick of tears. He grunted with transparent relief, and fumbled in his pockets. He was a tall thin man with a shiny bald pate fringed by an unruly thatch of grey hair. Despite Bridget's constant administrations he always appeared slightly creased and dishevelled. Even now a pale grey smear of ash decorated his shirt front.

'Found them!' he said after a minute, producing a box of matches. 'Now where's my pipe?' He looked around in bewilderment, then laughed. Frank and his pipe were rarely parted, though he mislaid it with remarkable regularity. After some hectic searching he located his beloved briar in his briefcase.

'How was Hong Kong?' Bridget asked as they sat down to dinner.

Frank twisted his lip. 'On the surface all goes well, but I'm unhappy. There's something fishy going on. It's all happened too easily. We've been assured we'll get the contract, that de Groots don't stand a chance, but why? They're very competitive.'

'Rory must be very pleased with himself,' Bridget commented.

'He's delighted. He's convinced the deal is as good as settled.' He turned to Leigh. 'Let me put you in the picture. The construction company we're negotiating with want to entirely re-equip. They have sites all over South-East Asia, so the outlay runs into millions of dollars. Tay Wong Chai, the owner of the firm, has recently retired and his three sons have taken control. We're dealing with Jimmy Tay, the youngest one.'

'And you don't trust him?'

'Not at all.'

'Why don't you ask Jake to speak with old man Tay?' Bridget suggested, spearing a piece of bright green okra. 'They're long-term friends.'

'Jake won't intrude. He's determined Rory should see the transaction through entirely on his own. Then all the glory, or failure, is his.'

'And if it's glory Rory will have convinced his father he's ready to take over as Chairman?"

'I suppose so.' Frank grimaced. 'Though personally I have some reservations about him. He's a very pleasant fellow, but not a hundred per cent committed to the company. He doesn't give it his undivided attention.'

'You mean he's not obsessed with work, like Jake?' Leigh said sharply, her grey eyes suddenly cold.

Frank and Bridget exchanged glances at her tone.

'I doubt Jake would work quite so hard if he had a wife to consider,' Frank said equably, 'but he doesn't. He directs all his energy into the company, and my goodness, he's been successful. The turnover has quadrupled in the past five years, mainly due to his efforts.

He pushes himself too far at times. He can look peaky.'

Leigh bit back an acid retort. She had never revealed her true feelings about Jake and his role in Patrick's death to the O'Briens. Now was not the time to enlighten them. It was better that the acrimony be forgotten.

'If Rory becomes Chairman how will Jake enjoy working for a man younger than he is?' she mused.

'Not much, I imagine.' Frank gave a dry laugh. 'They hardly see eye to eye at the moment.'

She felt a rush of malicious pleasure at his words. It would do Jake good to take orders from someone else. At present he was all-powerful. He was Sir Clive's blue-eyed boy, and was allowed an entirely free hand to run his part of the company as *he* thought fit. Apparently Rory would not be so acquiescent. Jake's mantle of self-assurance had always seemed invincible, she thought petulantly, it would be intriguing to see it torn aside.

'You were fortunate it was Jake who dealt with Patrick's death,' Frank commented, following through a train of thought which annoyed her intensely. 'He slashed through all the red tape like a scythe. You can't imagine what a hassle it was, dealing with the authorities. It went on for months, long after you returned home.'

Leigh studied her plate and made a non-committal murmur. If she told Frank and Bridget what she really felt about Jake she knew they would consider her unjust and ungrateful, so she preferred to leave them in ignorance. There was no need to resurrect violent emotions which were now carefully stifled. What was the point? Patrick was dead, there was no changing that. As far as the O'Briens were concerned she and Jake were still friends.

'And are you worn out already with Bridget's verbal diarrhoea?' Frank asked with a grin. His wife gave a shriek of protest which he ignored.

'I'm allowing her to rest, she's been down at the pool all day,' Bridget retorted in defiant justification.

Leigh laughed. 'I'm having a lovely time.'

The dinner plates were cleared, and a delicious cheese-cake brought on to the table.

'I thought tomorrow we'd go to the Botanical Gardens, then lunch at the club, and perhaps a quick look at the Crocodile Farm in the afternoon,' Bridget began to plan.

'Don't forget I'm not a proper tourist,' Leigh reminded her. 'I have been here before and seen some of the sights.'

'But things have altered since you were last here. Singapore's always changing—old buildings being pulled down and new ones going up. Besides, I'm sure you'd like to see everything again.'

Leigh was grateful for her concern, but Bridget did have a tendency to overdo things. As she feared, the following days were highly organised. She found herself being rushed through temples and mosques, museums and bird parks, with Bridget beside her, spouting endless information with all the dedication of a fully paid up member of the Tourist Guide Union.

'What have you planned for tomorrow?' Leigh asked, a couple of evenings later as they sat in the living room sipping liqueurs after dinner. It had been a hot and humid day, and her feet were burning after a lengthy walking tour of Chinatown.

'Nothing,' Bridget replied, much to her surprise. 'I hope you don't mind, but I always play bridge once a week with the girls.'

'*Girls!*' Frank exclaimed. 'Fifty years old each, if a day.'

'We usually have a morning session,' Bridget continued, patently dismissing his outburst, 'then break for lunch, and continue our game in the afternoon. Would you mind terribly if I deserted you for a day?'

'Not at all.' Leigh could hardly keep the pleasure from her voice. A day at a slower pace would be bliss.

'How about having lunch with me?' Frank puffed at his pipe.

'That would be nice.'

'Meet me at the office around noon, and I'll treat you to a slap-up meal. It's not only her ladyship who can live it up.' He winked and cast a wry look at his wife, but she was too busy thinking to retaliate.

'Don't forget to introduce Rory to Leigh,' she instructed, 'I told him she was coming. He said he'd be pleased to take her out.'

'He's not one of the young men you've inveigled into meeting me, is he?' Leigh asked with a groan.

'You'll adore him. *And* he's extremely eligible.'

'And if you interfere with his work, he'll cut out the work,' Frank added pithily, stretching foward to tap out his pipe.

'So what!' Bridget's eyes flashed, and Leigh realised her hostess had a soft spot for Rory. 'He doesn't want to be shut up in an office all day. He realises there's more to life than work. He likes to socialise.'

'He butters you up outrageously,' Frank derided with a grin, 'and you fall for it. You're just the same with Jake, he has you eating out of his hand, too.'

That was true, Leigh agreed silently, remembering how Jake had been utterly merciless when it came to chatting up Bridget. She had loved every minute, taking his teasing so seriously. He would tower above her, laughter glinting mischievously in his blue eyes, a twist at the side of his mouth, as she earnestly drank in his ridiculous stories.

'Where is Jake now?' she asked, not knowing why she wanted to know.

'Jakarta,' Frank supplied. 'See you about twelve noon tomorrow.'

The company offices occupied a suite on the nineteenth floor of a soaring glass-walled skyscraper which overlooked the faded red-tiled roofs of Chinatown on one side, and the wide stretch of the blue harbour on the other. Ancient and modern existed side by side, the new concrete giants of forty and fifty stories casting long shadows over the crumbling walls of decrepit godowns and shophouses. Progress, it was termed, as the heritage of Singapore was ruthlessly flattened to make way for more and more geometrically shaped office blocks, more and more shopping complexes. Only the river seemed eternal, a dark green shiny snake alive with bumboats and small craft as it slithered uncaringly among the old and the new.

Smoked glass doors slid silently apart to admit Leigh as she approached, and the slender heels of her strappy sandals tapped out a tattoo as she crossed the marble-floored lobby. The building was an architect's extravaganza, vast and elegant. Huge paintings, depicting the history of the island from the days of its founder, Sir Stamford Raffles, to the economic miracle of present times, hung from the walls. Crystal chandeliers sparkled iridescently in the high ceiling, and a bank of malachite green ferns tumbled discreetly from copper drums in a far corner. It was cool and quiet, with a rarefied atmosphere. Only the most prosperous companies could afford accommodation at such a prestigious address.

After spending the morning by the pool she had taken a leisurely shower, shampooed her hair and painted her nails. Already a golden glow shone from her skin, for she tanned easily, and several male heads swivelled to watch her progress towards the lifts. With the temperature zooming towards the nineties she was grateful she had decided to bring an ample supply of sundresses, though they had seemed ridiculously flimsy when she had packed them in the cold air of England. Her dress was of apricot-coloured cotton, its tight bodice accentuating her rounded curves. Shoestring straps tied on her smooth shoulders, and the full skirt swirled around her legs as she walked. She glanced briefly at the slender gold watch on her wrist. She had arrived a little too early to meet Frank. A light flashed and the lift doors opened, and a group of bespectacled Singaporean office workers emerged, chattering loudly, and walked away. For a moment it seemed as though she was destined to be the sole occupant of the lift, but as the doors began to slide together two muscular hands gripped them from the outside and forced them apart. They separated again, revealing a tall, strongly built man in his mid-thirties. He strolled casually in to join her.

'Jake!' she gasped, her eyes wide with surprise. 'I thought you were in Jakarta!'

CHAPTER TWO

'HELLO, Leigh. Welcome back. You look stunning as usual,' he replied, coolly bending his head to deposit a brief kiss on her cheek. She stiffened at the unexpected touch of his lips, her heart skidding as she eyed him suspiciously from beneath thick lashes. He had never kissed her before, not even socially. Indeed, he had always kept her very much at arm's length, which was unusual in this day and age when even mere acquaintances exchanged kisses as casually as proffering chocolates. Leigh was suddenly, overwhelmingly aware of the vibrant sexuality that simmered below the controlled façade he presented to the world. She bit her lip. Jake deposited his briefcase on the floor, then leaned back nonchalantly against the lift wall, folded his arms and studied her. 'Bridget told me you were coming to Singapore, but I didn't expect to meet you quite so soon,' he smiled. He was obviously pleased to see her, and she was surprised by his friendliness. 'I flew in only an hour ago. I've come straight from the airport.' Casually he began to look her up and down in bold appreciation, his eyes sliding almost insolently down from the torrent of silver-blonde hair, lingering over her slender body, until he reached the fine woven straps of her caramel-coloured sandals. 'Have you pressed the button?' he enquired laconically.

'Naturally.' Her reply was a trifle tart as she bridled beneath his gaze. She was accustomed to a glow of admiration in masculine glances, but usually they were more discreet. Jake's blatant manner unnerved her. It wasn't at all what she had expected. She could have coped with his anger, or cold indifference, but this outrageously sensual approach found her totally unprepared. He was assessing her critically, probably deciding if she would qualify for his harem, she judged

27

crossly as the lift moved upwards.

'Do I get marks out of ten?' she asked testily.

'I think an eight.' His amusement showed in an upward quirk at the corner of his mouth.

'Only an eight?'

'Eight is the most you can achieve by looks alone,' he explained with a grin. 'You win the two extra points by being good to the touch.'

Instinctively Leigh drew back. He had unknowingly hit upon a sensitive subject. Jake noticed the sudden tension in her face. He narrowed his eyes for a second, then abruptly steered the conversation in a different direction. 'Are you meeting Frank, or preparing to charm young Rory?' he asked with a faint trace of sarcasm.

'I have no intention of charming anyone,' she retorted, refusing to meet his eyes. Instead she devoted her attention to the indication lights as they lit up in turn.

'Bridget hasn't revealed her master plan yet?' He raised two thick mocking brows. 'Surely you realise an assignation between you and Rory was hatched up months ago? It will certainly make a change if Bridget's doing her matchmaking subtly this time. Now that you're in the market again she'll be arranging all kinds of delicious opportunities for you. Just pick the size, colour and age that appeals, and she'll produce a man to suit.'

'I'm *not* in the market,' she flashed him a blazing glance, furious at his assumption.

'Oh yes, you are,' he said firmly, touching the dark grey silk tie at his neck with long tanned fingers. 'The past is past. You don't have to forget it, but you can't live in it. How old are you now, twenty-five?' She gave a terse nod. 'Then it's high time you thought about getting married again. You're not a girl any more, you're a woman, and much too desirable to stay on the shelf. I'm surprised no virile young man has swept you off your feet by now.'

'I'm not interested.'

He glanced at her sharply. Leigh knew he didn't believe her, but it was true. It was safer not to fall in love again. Look what had happened the first time! She'd been so happy, so wrapped up in Patrick, and then her world had been ripped apart. She gave an involuntary shudder. She couldn't risk giving her heart so completely again—not yet, perhaps not ever. There was an unreadable expression in Jake's eyes as he surveyed her, and again he deftly switched the topic of conversation.

'Hellish hot to-day, isn't it, or perhaps I'm overdressed?' He tugged roughly at his tie in an effort to loosen the knot. He was immaculate in a charcoal grey three-piece pin-striped suit, with a pale grey silk shirt. For such an outspoken man he dressed in a decidedly conservative style.

'The waistcoat seems a little superfluous,' she commented.

'It is. I don't know why I wear it—habit, I guess. I must congratulate you on your outfit, there's certainly not too much of that.' His eyes dropped to her bare shoulders and the slight swell of her breasts above the taut bodice. She flushed. This provocative aspect of Jake's personality was new to her and profoundly disturbing. Hastily she looked down at the floor, then, avoiding the amusement in his eyes, transferred her gaze directly up to the indicator panel. The tenth floor light illuminated, then abruptly the lift shuddered to a stop and the lights snapped off. She gave a tiny squeak of dismay at the sudden blackness.

'Don't worry,' Jake's voice was calm. 'These lifts are always breaking down. Keep calm and I'll try to locate the emergency button.' He swore softly under his breath. 'I'm not sure which one it is, so cross your fingers and pray we don't shoot out of the roof.' She heard him fumbling with the switches. 'That should do it,' he said after a few seconds. 'The mechanics will be alerted, and with luck we shouldn't be marooned here for too long.'

She let out a breath of relief. As usual Jake was in complete control of the situation. It was maddening to feel grateful for his presence, but she couldn't avoid it.

'It feels as though the air-conditioning has broken down too,' he continued. 'It will become as hot as the fires of Hades in here in a few minutes. I'm going to remove a few layers. I presume you have no objection?'

'Go ahead,' she replied primly, acutely conscious of his invisible presence only a yard or two away in the pitch black. She was uncomfortably aware of the fact that the relationship between them appeared to have changed, and she couldn't understand why. Jake had initially been a good friend to both her and Patrick, but he had never once intimated that she appealed to him as a woman. His gaze today had brimmed with a sexual awareness which had knocked her well and truly off balance. He no longer regarded her merely as his colleague's wife. She was young and unattached, 'in the market' as he insisted, and it was undeniably apparent that he found her physically attractive. She bit again at the soft flesh of her bottom lip. Strangely, although his look had upset her, it had also stirred something within her, something she had presumed was dead. Jake was not a man to be ignored, with his direct eyes, firm jaw, and shock of thick, tawny-coloured hair that tumbled over his brow. His particular brand of infuriatingly confident masculinity did not appeal to her, she decided, but she could understand why other women waited in line for his favours. She drew a deep breath. A closer relationship with Jake was the last thing she wanted.

'Don't worry,' he drawled, as though reading her mind, 'I shan't seduce you, or would you prefer it if I did? I suppose it would pass the time.' Her face grew hot and she was grateful for the blackness which covered her confusion. His proximity was bothering her. 'I've removed my waistcoat and jacket, but I shall merely unbutton my shirt. I wouldn't want to tempt you.' The softly mocking voice made her pulses race. 'I only strip in lifts on Tuesdays, by special request, so I'm afraid you've missed your chance this week. Shame, isn't it?' He was laughing, deliberately baiting her.

'You stay in your small corner, and I'll stay in mine,'

Leigh suggested in what she hoped was a flippant manner.

'Yes, ma'am,' came the prompt reply, and she heard his heels click to attention. Already, as he had predicted, the temperature was soaring, bringing beads of perspiration to her face and arms. The air was stale. She felt a wave of dizziness and ran a hand across her damp brow.

'I'm going to sit on the floor,' Jake informed her through the blackness. 'You'd better join me, it'll be less tiring.'

Her legs felt weak and she quickly obeyed, leaning against the lift wall. 'Do you think we shall be trapped for long?' She tried, without success, to keep a tremor from her voice.

'We'll soon be on the move again,' he assured her gently. Suddenly the lift jolted. Leigh put her hands out flat on the floor to steady herself, her heart lurching with fear.

'Are you okay?' There was concern in his voice. 'Look, I know you said we should keep to our own corners, but I'd be much happier if we sat together, at least I'd know where you are. I'm coming across.'

She heard him moving towards her. His hand gripped her bare arm to locate her position in the darkness, and he sat down. His touch was strangely comforting and menacing at the same time. She could hear the steady rhythm of his breathing. Leigh swallowed hard, trying to think of something to say to break the heightened awareness of his presence beside her, an awareness which was threatening to choke her. 'Did your business go well in Jakarta?' she gabbled, the words coming out rushed and formal.

'Yes, thank you,' he replied in the same exaggeratedly polite tones. She moved her arm, but still he held it. The ball of his thumb began to rotate on her skin, sending danger signals into her nerve ends. 'I went to see my housekeeper's family,' he continued, much to her surprise. 'She has a sick child and I keep them informed of any progress.'

'Bridget told me about Choo.'

'And you, or she, or both, don't approve,' he said heavily.

'I didn't say that.'

'You didn't have to,' he flared. 'Your tone said it all.'

'But I've never even met her,' she protested weakly, embarrassed by his acute sensitivity.

'Precisely! Who needs facts when Bridget tells the tale? That woman deserves to be gagged—permanently. How on earth she imagines I'm unaware of her gossiping I'll never know.'

'Bridget's good at heart,' Leigh protested.

'I'll concede that. She's been very kind to Benjy, but she does love to tell tales out of school.'

'Only to her bridge friends.'

Jake snorted. 'Be realistic, Leigh. The first innuendo is only a pebble in a pool. Her bridge partners pass it on to their friends, who take it even further, and before you know it, there's a bloody tidal wave of slander. The British expatriate community here is small, as you know, rather like a village where everyone's madly interested in everyone else's affairs.'

'Especially yours?'

'Especially mine,' he agreed angrily. 'I suppose she also told you Choo's baby is illegitimate.'

'No. It was never mentioned,' she floundered, grateful to be able to relate the truth, even though she had presumed Choo was single.

'It will be,' he said frostily, removing his hand from her elbow. 'But believe me, there's no need for Choo to be married. She's better off unattached at present.'

Leigh didn't know what to say. Then there were distant sounds, a series of clicking noises, and the lift lights came on. She raised her hand to shield her eyes from the sudden glare.

'That's progress,' Jake smiled. Visibility had prompted a palpable change of mood in him, and the angry words in the darkness had apparently been forgotten. Wide, dark patches of sweat stained his shirt which was unbuttoned, revealing a tangle of damp black hairs on his muscular chest. A droplet trickled slowly down one side of his jaw and he pulled a white handkerchief from his trouser pocket to wipe it away. Then he reached across and solemnly wiped the moisture from Leigh's brow. The gesture was strangely tender and took her unawares. She smiled weakly, and he grinned, his blue eyes crinkling at the corners. Then she remembered his reputation as an experienced Romeo and moved away, suddenly wary.

'Have you a cigarette?' he asked, noting her withdrawal but making no comment on it, apart from a slight raise of his thick eyebrows.

'I don't smoke.'

'Of course not, I should have remembered.' He shrugged indifferently. 'So we can't smoke, I shan't continue my striptease, and you don't wish to be seduced, or so I presume?' He cocked a brow, but there was no response. 'Which only leaves small talk. Do you remember the last time we met?'

'Indeed I do.' Leigh looked away, her eyes quickly veiled. He watched her, aware of the tightness which had turned her full mouth into a hard, straight line.

'That was a long time ago, but time alters most things,' he said reasonably. 'I trust your ideas have changed. You're older now, you should have a more balanced view. You were extremely unreasonable before. I hope you've thrown away the blinkers.'

'You arrogant bastard!' she ground out, temper flushing her face. 'I was perfectly mature two years ago, and because my views differ from yours that doesn't mean they're unbalanced. If you hadn't been obsessed with that bloody company of yours Patrick would never have died!'

'You're being unfair,' Jake said harshly. 'He was like a brother to me. I was broken up when he had the accident.'

'I have no wish to discuss *your* feelings,' she sneered, 'so let's just forget it.' She turned from him, tilting her chin defiantly.

'*No!*' His reply sliced through the air like a machete.

'I want to clear the air—I must.' There was a note of desperation in his voice. 'I've lived with your unjust accusation for the past two years, now it's time for some home truths.'

'Leave it, Jake,' she ordered, glaring at him. 'I didn't come back to stir up the past. I know there's only one thing you really care about—Milwain International. Patrick came a poor second.'

'You cold-blooded little bitch!' he accused, his face darkening with emotion. 'How you delight in twisting the knife! Surely you must have wondered if your version of what happened could have been distorted, or are you so sure of your facts that there's no room for doubt?' He raked long fingers through his hair

'I know all the facts,' she cried impetuously. 'I know my husband is dead, what more is there to know?'

He looked across at her distressed profile. Her chin quivered and her large eyes filled with tears. 'Oh please don't cry,' Jake said.

'I'm not.' She blinked hard.

'I think we'd better call a truce, don't you?' He gave a sigh of resignation. 'I don't intend to spoil your holiday, and I certainly don't want Bridget and Frank to be aware of any bad vibrations between us.' He handed her his handkerchief. 'Here, blow your nose.' She did as she was told. 'I hope you'll come and see Benjy while you're over,' said Jake, impatiently snatching his glance from her unhappy expression. 'He still remembers you.'

'Of course I will,' she assured him, grateful that he had changed the subject, yet again. 'It must have been a wrench for him when your aunt left, I remember they were very close.'

'He was heartbroken, and so was she. But she found the climate exhausting, and I suspect Benjy was becoming too much of a handful. A small active boy is hard work for a woman in her sixties. She didn't want to leave, after all she'd looked after him since Melissa died. The parting was painful.' His face clouded.

'And now you have Choo.' Her voice was cautiously neutral.

'I have.' He twitched his nose. 'I don't know what Bridget's been saying, but the true facts are prosaic, despite her penchant for the dramatic. I'm very fond of Choo, she's been a good friend to Benjy and me. She offered to look after him when he was going through a very unsettled period of his life, and I shall always be grateful to her.'

The lift shuddered again, and Leigh held her breath and waited. When there was no further movement she sighed and leaned wearily against the wall. The humid air was clammy against her skin, like a wet, warm blancmange. Sweat ran down between her shoulder blades.

'Relax,' Jake said gently. 'Do you feel all right?'

'It's so airless,' she complained. 'I've never suffered from claustrophobia, but I'm beginning to understand the sensation.'

'Don't fret, my beautiful girl, we'll be rescued soon.'

'I'm not your beautiful girl,' she said witheringly, rankled by the patronising air of male benevolence which he had adopted.

'What a shame.' He dismissed her outburst with an eloquent gesture of his broad shoulders.

Leigh knew she had reacted badly, but the strain of being trapped in the enclosed space was beginning to play on her nerves. She was also uncomfortably aware that Jake possessed a maddening knack of bringing out the worst in her. She clenched her teeth. Why couldn't she remain cool and composed with him as she was with other men? He really was disturbing. Where had her calm indifference vanished to? Her emotions were no longer numb. He had provoked a seething irritation, his calm air of masculine superiority setting her nerves on edge. She didn't want to feel strongly ever again. To feel meant pain, and pain was to be avoided at all costs. If she could keep her emotions on an even keel, with no highs and no lows, then she would be safe. Her breasts rose and fell as she struggled to regain a measure of indifference.

Jake watched her closely, seeing more of her inner self than she realised. 'I believe you work as a secretary to some human dynamo?' he said at last.

'One of your kind,' she remarked coolly. 'Though he does find time to mow his lawn and wash his car at weekends.'

'I employ people to do that for me,' he said lightly, 'and what about men?'

'You mean boy-friends?'

With a backward jerk of his head he shook the thick fall of hair from his brow. 'No, I mean men. You're not a teenager any more, Leigh. You've been married. I don't imagine for one moment that a fumbled kiss on the doorstep from some callow youth would satisfy your needs.'

'I don't have any needs,' she snapped, her colour rising.

'Don't lie.' His voice was curt. 'At least have the decency to tell the truth, for heaven's sake! We all have needs. You don't have to deny them. Different people handle them in different ways, that's all.'

'Like you and your women!' Her disdain filled the air.

'Why do you choose to believe all those silly rumours Bridget spreads around?' he growled. 'There are some areas in which you show a remarkable lack of sense.' His nostrils flared with indignation. 'On the one hand you accuse me of being obsessed with work, and yet you maintain I lead a life gratifying my unparalleled lust. There are only twenty-four hours in the day—I can't possibly have time for everything, so which role do you prefer me to play? Really, for an intelligent woman you have some incredible blind spots.'

'How dare you!' Leigh lashed out impetuously with her hand in the direction of his face, but he had anticipated her move and firmly caught her wrist in mid-air. She was trembling with rage, rage at herself and at him. Slowly, quietly, he lowered her wrist and placed his hands on her shoulders. She felt the leashed strength inside him and avoided his eyes, dropping her gaze to the floor.

'Why must we fight?' he asked. 'The last time we saw each other we fought, and again now. I don't understand why.' She was surprised to detect a pang of despair in his voice, and glanced at him quickly through her thick, dark lashes. His expression was unreadable. He rubbed his brow savagely. 'Let's start again,' he said wearily, standing up and thrusting one hand deep into his trouser pocket. 'Are you lunching with Frank and Rory?'

'I believe so, but I wish Bridget hadn't arranged it.'

'You'll like Rory,' he commented drily. 'But don't get carried away by his boyish good looks and cavalier attitude.'

'You mean he doesn't work all the hours heaven sends?'

The jibe went home, and Jake flushed. 'He gets away with murder because he's charming *and* the Chairman's one and only heir. It's a privileged position.'

'Sour grapes?' she asked archly.

'No.' His tone was assertive. 'But I do believe in people fulfilling their responsibilities, and that's something Rory isn't too particular about. He's had a charmed life. He's the child of Sir Clive's old age and has always been indulged.'

'He'll take control when Sir Clive retires?'

'I imagine so. It is a family business, despite its size. The Milwains own the majority of the shares. The eldest son has taken over for the past two or three generations, but Rory will be the youngest Chairman ever. He's only thirty. Sir Clive should have retired years ago, but he's been waiting for Rory to gain enough experience.' His brows shot upwards in a look of pure irony.

Before Leigh could comment the lights flickered and there was a rush of cool air. Slowly, tentatively the lift began to rise, and she stood up. Jake put his arm around her shoulders as she staggered with the movement. The antagonism of their encounter was forgotten in their relief, and they both smiled at each other.

'Thank heavens for air-con,' Jake breathed. His face was damp and she noticed the sweat glistening among the dark hairs on his forearms. For an instant he held her close, then, as the movement of the lift became steady, he released her. She was thankful he had put some space between them, for the comforting strength of his arm was beginning to upset her equilibrium. His shirt was soaked; it clung to his firm chest and back like a wet rag. He slung his waistcoat and jacket over one arm and picked up the briefcase. Leigh fidgeted with damp strands of hair which lay limply around her shoulders, watching the buttons illuminate in turn—fifteen, sixteen, seventeen.

'I hope you enjoy your holiday,' Jake said slowly, putting his head on one side as he studied her. 'And I hope we can get along together without any more flareups! I promise I shall be on my best behaviour from now on.' His mouth lifted at one corner with a trace of humour. With sudden insight Leigh realised he had almost enjoyed their hot-blooded reunion.

'Fine,' she said decisively, 'that suits me.'

Not that the lift was moving again she was beginning to feel calmer and more in control of herself. Obviously her over-sensitive state could be attributed to the fraught dilemma of being trapped, and not to Jake's presence. The unconscious panic which had bubbled below her emotions was receding, and she was grateful for Jake's company. It would have been alarming to have been trapped in the darkened lift alone.

'Kiss and make up?' The mischief in his grin was irresistible, and she smiled.

'I consider a handshake is sufficient.' She offered a damp, sticky hand. With an elaborate bow he bent forward and lifted her fingers to his lips. He looked at her, a strange emotion flickering in the cool colour of his eyes. 'I've never kissed a sweatier hand!'

The lift reached its destination and he stood aside, allowing her to pass. Leigh stepped out on to the deep crimson carpet of the company offices. She felt an overwhelming relief at being free once more. Jake gave a deep sigh, making her wonder if his calm control had perhaps masked feelings of anxiety, then she dismissed the thought. He was far too self-assured to be discon-

certed by such a minor calamity. As she walked forward
along the hallway his strong fingers closed around her
upper arm. He pulled her to a halt, then swung her
round to face him. 'We deserve a stiff drink,' he
declared. The proprietorial touch of his fingers on her
skin vexed her. Did he imagine she was another weak-
kneed woman who would comply with his every whim?

'I don't want a drink, thank you,' she said flatly, pulling her arm from his grasp.

'You don't smoke. You don't drink. I can only presume you devote all your sinful energies to your sex
life.' He lifted a quizzical brow, and she stiffened. Why
must he continually insist on crediting her with sexual
attachments? Didn't he understand that that part of her
life was finished? Before she could snap out a suitably
sarcastic rejoinder to put him firmly in his place, swing
doors at the far end of the hallway were pushed open
and a willowy Eurasian girl in her early twenties
emerged. She stopped in surprise when she saw them.
'Mr St John! I didn't expect you back today. Surely
your return was scheduled for tomorrow? Did you have
a pleasant trip?'

'I worked overtime,' he said, with a sideways glance
at Leigh. 'I'm back early because I want to devote some
time to studying the job that's coming up in Taiwan. As
for the journey—well, the flight was on time, but Leigh
and I have been trapped in that confounded contraption
for the past forty minutes or so.' He tossed a careless
glance over his shoulder at the offending lift. 'Can I
introduce you? This is Mrs Nicholas, Patrick's widow.'

The girl stepped forward and delicately placed a cool
slender hand in Leigh's warm, damp one. 'I believe
we've met before,' she said. 'When Patrick worked here.
I'm Sunantha, Mr St John's confidential and personal
secretary.'

Leigh smiled a greeting. She was acutely aware of her
bedraggled appearance. Her hands were soiled from
steadying herself on the lift floor, and her dress was sad
and creased. In complete contrast the girl before her
was a vision of stylish elegance, from the top of her

sleek ebony head to her frivolously high heels. She wore an immaculate black taffeta two-piece, with a pure silk scarf in slashes of black and white at her neck. A huge brooch, in the shape of a golden orchid, was pinned to her lapel. Leigh tugged at her sodden curls, feeling gauche and awkward. 'Yes, I'm sure we've met before, at a company dinner or something.' Her voice trailed away. Already the girl had dismissed her and was turning solicitously to Jake, giving him the full benefit of her wide welcoming smile.

'Let me carry your briefcase and jacket, Mr St John. It must have been a terrifying experience to have been trapped for so long. You look quite damp and dishevelled—and you, too, Mrs Nicholas.' She cast Leigh a brief glance which indicated that whereas Jake was attractively tousled, she just looked a mess. Jake calmly handed over his case and coat as Sunantha hovered anxiously by his side, gazing up at him with large, limpid brown eyes. She was a striking girl, with pale amber skin and high cheekbones. She touched Jake's arm. 'Can I bring you a drink, or would you prefer to rest? I'll cancel all your phone calls to your office and then you can have some peace. I can send out for lunch if you prefer.'

Leigh pursed her lips. It's a wonder she doesn't offer to rush out and buy him a fresh change of clothes, she thought contemptuously. Jake saw her tight expression and smiled smugly. He appeared absolutely certain that this lavish admiration was no more than his due and basked happily in the glow of Sunantha's concern.

'Where can I find Frank?' Leigh asked briskly, moving forward. She had had enough of the master and willing slave routine. The way Sunantha fawned over her employer was nauseating, and his calm acceptance of the situation was even worse.

'At the end of the hallway, the door on the left,' Sunantha answered. 'If you care to wait a minute until I've organised a cool drink for Mr St John, I'll show you the way.'

'Please don't bother,' Leigh's voice dripped acid. 'You

must devote all your attention to him. He's been through a most disturbing experience, and I know he'll appreciate lots of tender loving care. I'll locate Mr O'Brien myself.' She turned smartly on her heel and walked away, leaving Jake staring wide-eyed after her.

Frank's large leather-topped desk was piled high with files, books and correspondence. He sat behind it, almost hidden by the chaos, pipe clenched between his teeth, engrossed in columns of figures on a foolscap sheet, his brow furrowed as he mumbled to himself beneath his breath. He looked up, startled at the sound of his office door opening, then his face cleared into a broad smile as Leigh appeared.

'And what happened to you?' he enquired in his Irish brogue, raising his eyebrows at her bedraggled appearance. 'You appear to have recently crossed the Sahara without the benefit of a camel.'

'I was trapped in the lift with Jake!'

'That's strange. I've never known of any problems with the lifts before.'

'He said they were always breaking down,' she protested.

'Probably trying to keep you calm. You look very hot and sweaty. Are you all right?'

She nodded.

'Then I suggest you freshen up in the washroom, my darlin', while I get you a long, cool drink. I presume Sunantha is tending to the boss's needs?'

'She certainly is,' Leigh retorted pertly.

The refreshing surge of cold water over her wrists was bliss, and she stood for several minutes, hands beneath the running tap, as she cooled down. She looked steadily at herself in the mirror. Jake's reaction to her needed consideration. Until Patrick's accident their relationship had been neutral and easy. It had never contained one grain of sexual awareness, at least not on her side. She had neatly slotted him into a pigeonhole in her life labelled 'husband's colleague', which meant he was sexless, and she presumed Jake had done the same with her. As long as she had been married she had been unaware of his animal magnetism, but now everything had changed. Leigh took a deep breath. Perhaps she was overreacting. The electricity which had flowed between them, uniting them and then jolting them apart, must surely be a figment of her imagination, only caused by the enforced intimacy of being trapped in the lift together.

The next time they met, it would be in an easier environment. After all, Jake was no different from any other man. Even if he was attracted to her he would soon get the message, like the others had. She dried her hands and wondered, briefly, how he had managed, so quickly, to penetrate the barrier she had erected. There was no doubt he had thrown her emotions violently out of focus, making her react instinctively. She dabbed at her face with a pastel pink tissue. The next time she met Jake, she decided determinedly, she would be casual, friendly, and on her guard.

Quickly she blotted her face dry, and renewed her blue-grey eye-shadow and mascara. Even with a touch of rosy lip-gloss the reflection in the mirror was hardly inspiring. Damp curls hung on her shoulders, and there were wet patches on her dress where she had tried to remove the worst of the dirty marks. She definitely did not look her best. It would be no surprise if Rory, her contrived date, took one glance and concocted a quick excuse for leaving, which would be something of a relief. If only Bridget didn't feel duty bound to provide escorts for her! Leigh straightened up and wrinkled her nose at herself. Perhaps she could persuade Frank to have a casual lunch, preferably out of doors where there was a chance of drying off in the noonday sun. She would be out of place in an expensive restaurant, with hovering waiters and a smartly dressed clientele.

'That's better.' Frank leaned back in his chair to smile at her. 'I can see your temperature has started to drop already, and a hearty swig of this lemonade should help reduce it even further.' He indicated a tall glass, liberally spiced with ice cubes. 'Just sit down there quietly for a few minutes, my darlin', and regain your cool.'

Leigh sank down gratefully in a studded leather arm-chair and took a long pull at the lemonade.

'I've buzzed through to Rory's office,' Frank con-tinued, sending a shower of ash over the desk as he gestured with his pipe, 'and it appears he's just stepped out. He'll be back in a few minutes. He whizzes through here like a tornado, I can never keep track of him. If he concentrated all his energies on the business, instead of the sports and social scene, he'd be another winner, like Jake.'

'It's not everyone who wants to be a super-efficient business executive one hundred per cent of the time.' Her tone was scathing.

'True.'

'I gather Jake doesn't entirely approve of Rory?'

Frank puffed at his pipe for a moment before reply-ing. 'Jake sets high standards. Fortunately Patrick was of a similar type, but Rory prefers to take life easier. Jake resents it.' He shrugged. 'Just a different outlook, I suppose.'

Leigh took a final sip of her drink as she considered his words. Jake's devotion to the company had certainly proved to be catastrophic in her life, she reflected bitterly. She set the empty glass down. 'That was good. I hadn't realised how parched I was. It tasted like nectar!'

'Can I get you another? There's plenty more in the fridge.'

'No, thanks. I'm fine now.' She walked over to the window. 'You have a fantastic view of the harbour from here. Those islands in the distance must be Indonesia?'

'That's right.' The reply came in an unfamiliar voice, and Leigh turned in surprise. A smiling young man with dark brown curly hair and a moustache had entered the office. He was trim in tailored beige slacks and a brown short-sleeved shirt.

'Darlin', can I introduce Rory Milwain,' said Frank from his desk. 'He's covering some of the areas Patrick used to deal with.'

Leigh extended a hand which was now, thank

heavens, cool and dry. 'Leigh Nicholas. As you probably know, Patrick was my husband.'

He grinned at her, ignoring the sweat-stained dress and soggy hair. He had friendly brown eyes. 'Delighted to meet you,' he said as though he meant it. 'I'm supposed to be Jake's right-hand man at the moment!' He turned to Frank. 'Have you got those prices for the Taiwanese job? I was intending to sort them out, but Jake's caught me on the hop. I didn't think he'd be back until tomorrow and he's been making enquiries about them.'

'They're here,' Frank confirmed, pulling a sheaf of papers from his desk drawer.

'Good. I'll deal with them after lunch.' He switched his eyes to Leigh. 'I was sorry to hear about Patrick. I met him a couple of times, he was a great guy.' He paused. 'How does it feel to be back in Singapore?'

'Fine. I'm enjoying all the sunshine.'

'She's just been trapped in the lift with Jake,' Frank intervened, 'hence the wet spaniel look!'

'Poor you. No doubt the boss is already making irate enquiries into the cause of the breakdown, and playing hell with some unsuspecting maintenance man.' Rory gave her a broad wink. 'Our Tuan Number One takes his, and other people's responsibilities, very seriously.'

'That's not a bad thing,' Frank pointed out.

'He's a slave-driver,' Rory spread his hands in mock despair. 'He should loosen up and live a little. I swear his idea of relaxation is to get on a plane with a pile of balance sheets to browse over.'

'And what's yours?' asked Leigh with a laugh, as Frank ushered the pair of them out of the door.

Rory gave a lopsided grin. 'To play rugby, or swim, or chat up a pretty girl.'

'So you're in your element now?' Frank queried, giving a meaningful glance at Leigh's pert profile.

'You bet!' he confirmed with a wide smile.

Frank closed the door behind him, and followed Leigh and Rory along the wide hallway. Large glossy photographs of earth-moving equipment—diggers and dumpers—were displayed on the pine-panelled walls. To the left was a heavy door which announced, 'J. St John—Generai Manager and Director', in imposing gold letters. As they approached it was flung open and Jake emerged. He, too, had obviously had a wash and brush up for he looked much fresher, though his dark hair still curled damply over his collar. He had changed into a crisp pale blue poplin shirt, and Leigh wondered, disparagingly, whether Sunantha had a supply of brand-new shirts neatly stacked in a drawer somewhere, ready for such a sartorial emergency. The girl had stressed that she was Jake's *confidential* secretary, and presumably confidential included buying his clothes and all kinds of other personal matters. Leigh refused to think further.

'Frank, Rory,' Jake nodded at the two men. 'Off to lunch?' His cool blue eyes barely skimmed Leigh.

'Want to come along?' Frank asked casually, taking his pipe from his mouth, and Leigh tensed. She had had enough of Jake's disturbing presence for one day. He cast her a sharp glance. 'No, thank you. There's a stack of mail and telexes a mile high which requires my attention. Sunantha and I will be burning the midnight oil if I don't start on them immediately.' Leigh gave an inward sigh of relief. 'Incidentally,' he continued, turning to her, 'I've just had a word with the maintenance staff. It appears a fool of an engineer decided to do some minor repair work on the lift before checking that it was unoccupied. It won't happen again. He's been strongly reprimanded.' Leigh was aware of Rory winking at her from behind Jake's shoulder. 'It could have been unfortunate,' Jake continued solemnly. 'If an old person had been trapped in the dark it might have triggered off a heart attack or hysteria.'

Rory gave a smothered grunt of hilarity, and Jake glanced at him, his eyes like cold steel. 'It's no laughing matter,' he said sharply.

'You were trapped in the lift with a gorgeous young woman, you lucky devil,' Rory burst out. 'I bet you were too busy trying to get to grips with her in the dark to succumb to coronary arrest!'

For a moment Jake looked unexpectedly nonplussed, then his handsome face darkened. 'Have a good lunch,' he said heavily.

Fortunately the lift arrived before the animosity between the two men could develop further. As Rory and Frank strode forward Leigh felt Jake's fingers on her wrist, forcing her back. 'Just remember Rory's a lightweight,' he muttered into her ear. 'He might have been around and about, but he hasn't had much heavy experience like you and me.'

She snatched her arm from his grasp and marched into the lift. The inference in his voice made her pulses race, and she stared defiantly back at the sardonic mockery in his eyes until the doors slid together and he disappeared from view.

CHAPTER THREE

LUNCH was fun. Frank was perfectly content to fall in with Leigh's preferences—anything for a quiet life. He took the young couple to an open-air café on the quayside, only a few minutes' walk from the office, and as they strolled beneath the blaze of the tropical sun Leigh's dress began to dry and her hair regained some of its natural bounce. They found a table in the shade of a palm tree, overlooking the deep greeny-blue waters where lighters plied to and fro between ocean-going ships anchored out in the harbour, and godowns crowding the banks of the Singapore River. The lighters had wide wooden hulls and rode low in the water, carrying their heavy cargoes of rice, rubber or grain. On every prow a pair of all-seeing eyes was painted.

'The eyes are to enable the boats to see where they're going and avoid collisions. It's an old Chinese custom,' Frank explained.

'They should paint eyes on cars too,' Rory said with a grin, 'and eliminate road accidents!'

A friendly Malay girl in a colourful batik sarong kebaya brought menus, and after Frank had ordered beer for himself and Rory, and fresh lime juice for Leigh, they settled down to the happy chore of deciding what to eat.

'I'd love to try Szechuan prawns again, please,' Leigh decided, 'they're so big and tasty here, not at all like the tiny frozen ones you can buy at home.'

'That would suit me, too,' Rory agreed. 'How about you, Frank?'

The older man pulled a wry face at their choice. 'Steak and chips for yours truly. You can't beat a good cut of meat, decently cooked. Wait until you've lived abroad as long as I have, all these exotic foods begin to pall.

Make the most of your fish-head curries and shark's fin soups now, because I guarantee eventually you'll return to meat and two veg.'

It was pleasant sitting in the warm, humid breeze watching the dazzle of the sun on choppy little waves and the activities of the wiry, brown-bodied boatmen as they loaded their multifarious cargoes. Rory was easy to talk to. He had a lighthearted sense of humour, and Leigh relaxed. The conversation flowed easily between the three of them and she wondered why, in contrast, her meeting with Jake had been so spiked with emotion. He was a complex character. Idly she wondered if he, too, had built up a barrier to protect his vulnerability, for his life had had its share of disasters. It was rare for Jake to reveal his innermost feelings. He was inevitably in tight control of himself. The public man was always so self-assured; it would be intriguing to catch a glimpse of the private man. Or would it? Jake's annoying magnetism had already unsettled her. It would be plain foolish to become further embroiled. She was grateful that Rory exhibited a straightforward friendliness which contained no undercurrents. He flirted happily with her, and she fell into his mood, laughing as he related one comical anecdote after another.

'You've been around,' Frank commented, pushing aside his empty plate and settling back to light his pipe.

'I was based in South America for a couple of years before I came East,' Rory explained. 'My father wants me to have as wide an experience as possible.'

'I believe you're in the process of clinching an important contract in Hong Kong,' Leigh smiled.

Rory nodded. 'I don't anticipate any problems. My father is coming out to Singapore in a couple of weeks' time, and if everything could be finalised by then I'd be delighted.'

Frank began to doze in the balmy heat. Leigh cast an affectionate glance at his drooping eyelids and exchanged a smile with Rory as they watched him slide into sleep.

'Do you play many sports?' she asked. Rory looked

like an athlete, brimming with vitality and good health.

'Squash, tennis, badminton, weekly rugby, and when there's time I like to windsurf and water-ski. How about having a game with me some time?'

'A game of what?' she asked archly, wondering how it could feel so safe to flirt with Rory, while a simple conversation with Jake had her struggling out of her depth. It didn't make sense.

'We could try tennis for a start,' he grinned, 'and move on to some other form of amusement later.' The double meaning was apparent from his expression. They chatted idly, sipping their cool drinks, until Frank jerked himself awake with a sudden start, and glanced guiltily at his watch. 'Come on, you two, it's almost three. Jake'll be sending out a posse.'

'Another black mark,' said Rory with an unashamed grin. 'I shall tell him Leigh led us astray.'

'Don't you dare!' she retorted with a laugh.

'I'll phone you later this afternoon to fix up the tennis,' he promised as they parted company in front of the office block. The two men vanished through the glass doors, and Leigh smiled. The prospect of a date with Rory was distinctly pleasing, even if Bridget had worked furiously behind the scenes. He was fun to be with, and *safe*, that was the main thing. She knew instinctively that she could control any friendship which might develop between them, and perhaps this time she was ready for something stronger. She lifted her brows. Returning to Singapore seemed to have triggered off a new phase. Leigh pivoted on her heel and walked smartly across the white-painted iron footbridge which spanned the river. There was a smile on her lips as she waited at the taxi stand. The Chinese taxi driver who took her back to the apartment spoke limited English, but he tried his best to talk to the happy girl, and they managed to communicate, after a fashion, with much waving of hands and laughter.

Bridget returned home later that afternoon, and after describing at great length the many hands of bridge she had played, demanded to be given a blow-by-blow ac-

count of Leigh's day. She was horrified to hear of the
interlude in the lift. 'I should have become quite hysterical,' she declared, pressing her hands to her ample
bosom in wild agitation. 'I couldn't bear being trapped
in the dark, especially suspended ten flights up. Suppose
the cable had snapped, or there'd been a fire?' She
looked panic-stricken at the thought.

'The breakdown wasn't that serious,' Leigh assured
her with a smile. Bridget's reaction had immediately
placed the event on a par with a key scene from a disaster movie. 'We were perfectly safe. Jake was calm—he
didn't think we were in any danger. His attitude
probably kept me from worrying.'

'If you have to be trapped in a lift then the best companion must be Jake,' Bridget said knowingly. 'He's
always super cool and efficient. He knows what to do
for the best. He makes you feel safe. Mind you, I can
think of plenty of young women who wouldn't want to
be rescued if they were trapped in the dark with him.'
She flashed Leigh a glance. 'But he always treats you
like a kid sister, doesn't he?'

Leigh made no comment. Jake would certainly not be
her first choice of a companion, and as far as feeling
safe—she had felt decidedly threatened, though she
couldn't decide exactly *what* it was she had been wary
of. Swiftly she changed the subject and described her
meeting with Rory.

'What do you think of him?' asked Bridget eagerly.
'Wasn't I right? Isn't he a lovely young man?'

'He's very nice.' Leigh gaveman inward groan as the
older woman moved closer to her on the sofa, eager to
hear about every topic they had discussed, every
mouthful they had eaten. Bridget's interest was ex-
cessive. It seemed as though she was mentally computing
everything away in order to repeat it at a later date.
Leigh had no idea why a stranger should be interested
in her actions. Merely a case of idle tongues, she
presumed. If Bridget had a hard day's work to do, she'd
have neither the time nor the inclination to gossip. It
was a relief when the shrill ring of the telephone inter-

rupted their conversation and Bridget jumped up to answer it. 'For you,' she hissed theatrically, her hand over the mouthpiece. 'It's Rory. He wants to play tennis. He must be telepathic, phoning when we were discussing him!' She handed over the receiver and returned to her seat, keeping an interested ear on the conversation.

'Fancy tennis this evening?' Rory asked.

'That would be fine, but where?' Leigh became aware of Bridget flailing her arms wildly in an attempt to attract her attention.

'Tell him to come and play here,' she insisted in a piercing stage whisper. 'There are two simply beautiful courts downstairs in the grounds, and I can easily book one for you.'

'I heard that,' Rory's voice brimmed with amusement. 'Please thank Bridget for me, that would be fine.' When the three-sided phone call was over it had been arranged for Rory to arrive straight from work in an hour's time.

'You could play later,' Bridget mused. 'The courts are floodlit, but I believe mosquitoes can be a problem at dusk and when it gets dark.' She fingered the jade beads at her neck thoughtfully. 'You can both shower up here after your game. Then perhaps he'll take you out to dinner, or do you think I should invite him to eat with us?'

Leigh held up her hands in supplication. 'Just leave things alone,' she pleaded.

Bridget was pushing too hard. 'My guess is he'll take you to dinner,' she decided, barging along cheerfully with all the sensitivity of a piledriver. 'I told him it wasn't right for you to be cooped up with two old fuddy-duddies like Frank and me.'

'You shouldn't have done that!' Leigh gave a wail of dismay. 'You're about as subtle as a shillelagh! It's embarrassing to have prearranged dates.'

'I don't want you to be bored with life.'

'I'm not!'

'Besides, Jake agreed that a change of scene, a touch of sunshine, the chance to meet new people, would be therapeutic for you.'

'He did, did he?' commented Leigh drily.

'He always wants to hear how you're getting along.
I've shown him your letters.'

Leigh tightened her lips in a flash of pique. How dared
he check up on her? Why the hell couldn't he keep out
of her life? He'd caused enough trouble already.

Although it was after five when Leigh and Rory
started their game the temperature was in the nineties
and the humidity was high. Tall casuarina trees shaded
the courts from the worst of the sun's glare, but Leigh
still found herself flushed and panting within minutes.
'Let me have a drink, Rory,' she pleaded laughingly, at
the end of the first set. 'You've worn me into the ground!
I'd forgotten how hot it is here, and how much of an
effort it is to run around in the sun.' She mopped her
brow with a white towel and briskly wiped her tanned
limbs. She looked neat in a crisp white tennis dress, the
neckline and armholes edged in navy. Her hair was
pulled back into two gleaming bunches which protruded
from beneath a white peaked cap. Rory pulled the ring
tabs on two cans of fizzy cola and handed one to her as
they took a well-earned rest. 'It's a great setting, isn't
it?' he commented, looking around at the spacious
grounds. 'The gardeners here do a fine job, and the
courts are well maintained. They must put in a lot of
hours.'

'I've seen them dragging a roller across the shale first
thing in the morning,' Leigh confirmed. 'The pool's well
cared for too.' They looked over to the azure blue water
where children were still splashing happily, their shouts
drifting across on the scented evening air. A pair of
golden orioles soared towards the trees to settle on a
high branch.

'Come on.' Rory was impatient to be playing. 'Let's
see if I can trounce you once again before the sun starts
to go. It'll be dark by seven, so we'd better get a move
on.'

The evening light had begun to fade as they reached
the final game and Leigh acknowledged an easy defeat.
It came as no surprise when he suggested they dine to-

gether. 'You're obeying Bridget's instructions!' she re-monstrated.

'Not really,' he protested with a grin. 'Believe me, if you'd been hideous I'd have invented some immediate excuse to ditch you, but as you're . . .' He paused.

'Not hideous?'

'Simply gorgeous,' he amended, slipping his arm around her waist as they walked from the court. 'I'm delighted to go along with her plans. She's provided me with an unbelievable array of females in the past—the good, the bad and the downright ugly. However, on this occasion I'm full of admiration.'

Leigh grinned. She silently agreed that her hostess's matchmaking was not too catastrophic after all.

Bridget flapped around offering drinks and abundant hospitality when they returned to the apartment. They exchanged amused glances at her behaviour before dis-appearing for their respective showers. After a refreshing plunge under the cold water Leigh shampooed her hair and quickly blow-dried it before changing into a filmy gold and white flowered dress with long full sleeves and a softly flowing skirt. Tiny pears were fastened into her ears, and she wore a pearl drop on a fine gold chain around her neck. The image in the mirror was a vast improvement on the soggy apparition Rory had first encountered. He was already waiting, freshly scrubbed and shining, his hair still damp from the shower, when she joined the others in the living room. He broke off his conversation with Frank, and rose to greet her, the warmth in his eyes telling her she was beautiful.

'Take a key, dear,' Bridget fussed. 'Don't worry about what time you come home. Frank and I will be in bed, but you won't disturb us.' She was unable to hide a triumphant smile. 'Have a good time.' She picked an imaginary speck of lint from Rory's jacket. 'Drive care-fully,' she told him. 'Don't go too fast.'

'For heaven's sake,' Leigh raised her eyes to the ceil-ing in mock despair, 'we're not teenagers!

'I feel I should apologise for Bridget,' she said with a

smile as they entered the lift. 'She's like a mother hen fluttering around.'

'It's not your fault. She's a born do-gooder, that's all,' Rory laughed. 'She can't resist interfering, always in everyone's best interests, of course. She tries to pair everyone off, but don't worry—I'm used to it. She's not had much success so far, has she? I'm still single, and look at Jake—he continues to play the field, and she's been trying to marry him off for years. Mind you, any girl who took Jake on would have to be made of strong stuff.' They reached the car park. He opened the door of his red sports car and Leigh climbed in.

'What do you mean?' She was annoyed to find herself interested in the reply, for she had meant to banish all thoughts of the irritating Mr St John from her mind.

'He's a hard man. If you don't match up to his ideals he dismisses you.'

'But he's had a rough deal.' Leigh clipped on her seat-belt as the car moved forward and wondered why she, of all people, should be defending Jake. 'His wife died just after Benjy was born. Jake's had to bring him up alone. It can't have been easy.'

'I suppose not,' Rory admitted grudgingly. 'Certainly when I came here eighteen months ago he was in a dreadful state. I think Patrick's death revived some of the trauma he experienced over his wife. Bridget made him go to the doctor's for a check-up. He was very highly strung, very tense, and I reckon he was heading for a breakdown.'

'I didn't know that!' she frowned.

'He went around under a heavy black cloud for ages, but as you can see he's all right now. Jake always recovers.'

Leigh sat in silence as they drove along the busy city streets, her thoughts whirling. It had never occurred to her that Jake would be so distressed. At the time of Patrick's death she hadn't cared a toss about his feelings, she'd been far too engrossed in her own. It had been all too easy to imagine he had no weak spots, that he could cope no matter what happened, but perhaps she was wrong. She gave herself a mental shake. Why was she wasting sympathy on him? *He* was responsible for Patrick's accident, even if he did deny it.

'Are you looking forward to seeing your father?' she asked Rory as they pulled on to the forecourt of a large hotel.

'Very much—he's a great old boy. I'd desperately like the Hong Kong deal to be tied up by then. It'll give him a real boost to know I've achieved it all on my own. He'll be able to retire with a happy heart.'

'And you'll be Chairman?'

'I imagine so, though he's never said anything officially. Can't say the idea thrills me, but it's a family tradition.'

'You'll be based in London?'

Rory handed the car keys to the parking valet, and they entered the hotel lobby.

'I will, but I shall curb the mighty Jake St John, even from that distance.'

His tone was dangerously unpleasant, and Leigh widened her eyes a fraction in surprise. The affable good humour had momentarily been swept aside and the angles of his face were mean. She was seeing an unsuspected side of his character. Beneath the boyish charm lay a gritty streak of determination.

'I have to kowtow to him at present, but wait until *I'm* the boss, I'll make the bastard jump!'

Leigh felt uneasy at the threat in his voice. He sounded vindictive, as though thirsting for revenge, but then, as swiftly as it came, the moment passed.

'I hope you enjoy French food?' Rory gave her a smile as they walked into the restaurant with its red and white check tablecloths, and Leigh began to wonder if she'd imagined the note of bitterness.

'I love it,' she assured him as the waiter led them to their table.

The menu was expensive and the food delicious. They enjoyed a leisurely meal, the two-way conversation never flagging between them, and Leigh was happy to agree when Rory suggested they take in a disco. It was almost two in the morning by the time he returned her to the apartment.

'That was a great evening,' he told her as she fumbled in her bag for the key. 'How about going out again tomorrow? Same format? No doubt Bridget will be delighted to book a tennis court for us.' He lifted a brow. 'She'll be pleased to know her plans are working.'

'I'm sure she will.' Leigh's eyes sparkled with laughter. 'And perhaps tomorrow I shall beat you, or at least mark up a more respectable score.'

'You bet!' He gave her a soft kiss on the mouth. 'See you tomorrow, around five.'

It was noon the following day when he telephoned to cancel their date. 'It's Jake's fault,' he stormed. 'He's been through the Taiwan deal and says he wants more information. He's determined I should fly to Taipei this afternoon and set up some meetings.'

'Never mind,' she said gently, trying to pacify him.

'I do mind. It could wait. The matter isn't urgent, and I've told him so,' he replied hotly. 'It means I shall be away until the end of the week.'

'I'll see you at the weekend.'

'But I wanted us to be together this evening, and tomorrow. I'm tempted to tell him to go to hell and stay here regardless,' he grumbled. ' 'Struth, you're only here for a month, and Jake's ruining it all. Why should I obey his stupid demands?'

'He is the boss,' Leigh pointed out.

'I suppose so.'

Eventually, after much complaining, Rory calmed down, and rang off after fixing a date for his return.

Bridget was preparing lunch in the bright kitchen and heard the news of his imminent departure with tragic sighs. Then she cheered up. 'Shall I telephone my friend Sylvia? Her son's in town. He's been divorced, but he's only about thirty-eight, and is very suave.'

'No, thank you,' Leigh said firmly. 'No, no, no!'

After a salad lunch Bridget decided they would visit the orchid gardens in the north of the island. It was a beautiful day. The sun shone high in a cloudless sky, and a lazy breeze indulgently stirred the paper-dry blossoms of pink and purple bougainvilleas which grew in dragon pots around the balcony. After washing up the lunch dishes the two women departed to their rooms to change. Leigh picked out a loose cotton batik sundress in lavender and white. She slipped her bare feet into white high-heeled mules, and brushed her hair back into a bouncy ponytail before going into the living room to wait. As usual Bridget was taking ages to dress. Leigh could hear her talking to herself in the bedroom, and there was the sound of cupboards and drawers being rapidly opened and closed as she deliberated over which outfit she should wear. Leigh was leafing through the daily paper when the telephone rang.

'Can you answer that, darlin'?' Bridget called from the bedroom door, her hands thick with tinted foundation. She smeared some on her cheek and waited to discover the identity of the caller.

'May I speak with Mrs Nicholas, please?' a cool voice enquired.

'Speaking.' Leigh gestured that the call was for her, but Bridget still hovered in the doorway.

'This is Sunantha, Mr St John's secretary. I'm afraid he's tied up at a meeting and is unable to speak to you himself, but he asked me to ring and invite you to dinner at his home this evening.'

Leigh's temper rose. So Jake had been too busy to bother to pick up the telephone and speak to her himself, had he? As usual business came first. Well, she was damned if she was going to accept!

'Thank you, but . . .' she began, hurriedly composing a polite refusal.

'Who is it?' Bridget hissed. Leigh's stomach gave a sickening lurch. How could she possibly reject the invitation with Bridget listening in? The older woman knew she had no other plans and would consider it downright rude if she turned down dinner with Jake. She sighed impatiently. There was no way out; it was better to keep the peace. 'Thank you, and I'd be pleased to accept,' she amended with feigned grace. 'What time?'

'Mr St John says to be ready at eight. He'll collect you from the O'Briens' apartment.' The secretary was super-cool, her voice giving nothing away. Leigh wondered if she was jealous, but why should she be? Jake was only being socially correct. Her husband had been one of his employees, after all. Common politeness called for some gesture of hospitality on his part.

'Isn't that thoughtful?' Bridget beamed when she heard of the dinner date. 'He doesn't want you to be neglected while Rory's away.'

Leigh grunted. The last thing she needed was Jake's magnanimity.

As they drove rapidly along leafy, sunlit lanes to the orchid gardens she tried to convince herself that her feelings of trepidation were unfounded. Jake had always been perfectly correct when she had met him in the past, he was hardly likely to leap on her now. Or was he? The way his eyes had roved over her body in the lift had been provocative to say the least. Leigh shifted uncomfortably. She had a premonition that their relationship was destined to shoot off in a direction she could not control, and it frightened her. Was it possible he had purposely ordered Rory to Taiwan in order that she would be free that evening? Impatiently she thrust aside the speculation. She was flattering herself. Jake wouldn't know of their date. Besides, there was no way he would waste company time and money sending Rory on a futile journey; he kept a shrewd eye on all company expenditure and would be unwilling to push anyone off on a doubtful errand. Jake was a hardheaded executive; he would never use the company for his personal indulgence. Leigh gave herself a mental ticking off; she was making too much of his dinner invitation, but the prospect of being with Jake continued to grate.

The tropical sun was high when they reached the gardens, and Leigh was grateful for her dark glasses and sunhat. The orchids were planted in abundant rows, stretching far away up the hillside, their delicate beauty seeming at odds with the fleshy, dull green roots from which they grew.

'Have you been here before?' Bridget asked as they

walked up the grassy bank between the ranks of white, purple and golden blossoms.

'Once. Jake brought Patrick and me when we first came to Singapore.'

She remembered, somewhat reluctantly, how kind Jake had been when they arrived. He had unreservedly welcomed them both, and taken endless trouble to ensure they rented a pleasant apartment, and found an amah and a car. He had personally pulled strings to speed delivery of their shipment of personal goods from the docks. He had done everything in his power to help them settle down quickly. And his power was impressive; as head of the Far Eastern headquarters of an international company he had status. He was in a position of unthreatened authority. When Jake said 'jump' everyone jumped. Especially Patrick, she thought grimly, though Jake had always appreciated her husband's work. The relationship between them had been a close and satisfying one. She had admired Jake in those days, and had been proud that he and Patrick worked so well together. She felt a prickle of anger. In retrospect it would have been far better if Patrick had been more like Rory, not so eager to fall in with Jake's wishes. A soft sigh escaped her lips as she paused to examine an exotic creamy-coloured flower.

It was when her husband had started to travel that the trouble flared. Jake had carefully organised Patrick's first months in Singapore. He knew from his years in the East that it takes time for the European to adjust to the climate, the pace of life, the air travel. Patrick had worked in the office for the first two months, learning all he could about the Asian market, and gradually he had taken control of sales in Taiwan, Indonesia and the Philippines. Jake dealt with all the other countries, from Japan in the north down to Papua New Guinea in the south, a vast area covering thousands of miles. He also supervised Patrick's area, giving help and attending crucial meetings.

At first Patrick had professed to enjoy the travelling, for he was often on the move, but as months passed Leigh noticed taut lines of strain around his dark eyes.

An unhealthy pallor seeped into his face. The many hours in the air, waiting at crowded airports, eating strange foods at strange hours, began to take their toll.

'Tell Jake you need a rest,' Leigh had demanded one evening as Patrick sat wearily at the dinner table.

'Don't be ridiculous,' he had said. 'He works as hard as I do. He travels far more. I'm only finding it a strain because I'm new to the job, but I'll settle down. Jake's already applied to London for two new sales reps, then the pressure will ease. Heaven knows when they'll arrive though! Headquarters takes ages to give the go-ahead.'

Silently Leigh began to blame Jake. He should have anticipated the situation and arranged for extra staff to be waiting in the wings to cope with the intensified work load. But then Jake ran a tight ship, she had thought peevishly, he'd never carry staff who were not fully utilised. Patrick continued to brush aside her worries, and she had to admit that even when he was at home he refused to rest. He insisted they accept all invitations for cocktail parties and dinners which came their way, and totally rejected her attempts to make him take life at a slower pace.

'We're only here for a short time and it's a great social life,' Patrick had pointed out. 'Let's enjoy it while we can.'

To make matters worse, he contracted a virus and was racked with sickness. One day he had arrived home and collapsed on the bed. Hastily Leigh had telephoned the doctor who, after a quick examination, had ordered Patrick to stay in bed for a full week. The following Monday he had been off again, full of apologies to Jake for not pulling his weight. She grimaced at the irony. If Jake hadn't demanded so much Patrick would never have been ill. He found it difficult to shake off the lethargy which followed the virus, but reported that Jake was endeavouring to reduce his travel programme and that the pressure would soon lift. To Leigh there seemed little difference. Her husband continued to arrive home pale and weary. She curled her lip when she remembered the concern Jake had shown. He had apologised to her because Patrick continued to travel. His excuses had fallen on deaf ears. By then she had realised that only one thing really mattered to Jake St John—the profit the company made.

'Let's have a wee rest,' Bridget suggested as they reached the top of the bank. She was panting heavily, her face bright pink. 'It's quite a climb up here.' They found a stone seat overlooking the acres of colourful orchids and the hazy green hills of Malaysia in the distance. Vivid blue kingfishers swooped among the trees as Leigh raised her face to the sun. 'I love this heat.'

'You young people!' Bridget grumbled. 'Sunworshippers, the lot of you. Jake's always off in his speedboat at weekends with Benjy, and Rory's continually out in the sunshine. No wonder they're brown as berries. I just go puce!' She turned down her mouth in disgust. 'Wouldn't it be wonderful to have skin like Sunantha's, naturally light brown, and no need to bake in the glare of the sun to achieve it.'

'She's a lovely girl.'

'Jake thinks so, too. He takes her away on business trips sometimes.'

'She seems besotted with him,' Leigh remarked coolly.

Bridget snorted. 'All Asian woman are like that. They set up their men as idols.'

'I imagine Jake doesn't complain.'

'He enjoys having beautiful women around,' her hostess confirmed. 'All this subservience isn't good for him. He takes it for granted. He needs a woman who'll answer back.'

'Someone to slap his face for him occasionally?'

Bridget nodded.

'Won't Choo resent him asking me to dinner?' Leigh wondered aloud.

Bridget stood up and brushed at her skirt with beringed fingers before they retraced their steps down the hillside. 'I don't expect she has much choice. After all, he's the boss. She'd never dare to argue with him. She just has to accept his infidelities.'

'I'm hardly an infidelity,' Leigh retorted hotly.

'That's true, but even if you were Choo would have to accept it. She'd just wait for Jake to return to her.'

'Master and slave,' Leigh muttered under her breath.

Just like his relationship with Sunantha. Well, one thing was certain, he would soon discover Leigh Nicholas wasn't prepared to be anyone's slave.

That evening she chose her outfit with care. Jake was always immaculate. He would not be impressed if she turned up in baggy jeans and a tee-shirt. After a great deal of deliberation she decided upon a strapless dress in silk chiffon. It was black with a delicate pattern of mint green and sorrel-shaded flowers, and had a matching floral jacket in the same colours. She knotted her hair into a heavy, gleaming chignon at her neck and clipped tiny golden hoops into her ears. Deftly she applied pearly green shadow to her eyelids and a touch of blusher to emphasise her high cheekbones. When she studied herself in the mirror she felt well equipped for comparison with any Oriental lady.

'You look very pretty, dear,' Bridget smiled as she emerged from the bedroom. 'Have you got the key?'

Leigh nodded briefly. She hoped Bridget wasn't going to fuss again. Jake would take masculine delight in the embarrassing mother hen routine. She squirmed uncomfortably. This evening she wasn't embarking on a date with a friendly young admirer like Rory, instead she was dining with a mature man, who was a notorious ladykiller and who, it had to be admitted, was extraordinarily attractive.

Promptly at eight the doorbell rang. Frank glanced up from his book as Bridget bounded over to fling the door open wide. Jake had brought Benjy with him, and Leigh took a sharp breath at the sight of them together, framed in the doorway. Benjy was a miniature version of his father. The baby plumpness she remembered had fallen away, and the little boy had the same direct eyes, the same determined jaw. His small hand was in Jake's large one, and it was instantly apparent they shared a close relationship.

'Hello, my beautiful girl.' There was a laughing challenge in Jake's look as he released Benjy's hand and strode towards her. With a swift movement he put a firm hand behind her head and pulled her towards him.

He kissed her hard on the mouth, his lips lingering a moment too long, then stepped back and studied her. Leigh raised her fingers to her lips in bewilderment. The intimacy of the unexpected kiss had around a sudden, searing need. She was trapped in his steady gaze, not knowing what to say or do. Slowly his lips curved into a smile and instinctively she responded. For a long moment they were caught in a private spell, oblivious of everyone else in the room. Then Leigh deciphered a touch of triumph in the curl of his mouth and hurriedly remembered his reputation. She stiffened, her features hardening into a subtle rejection. Jake looked puzzled, disconcerted by her change of mood, and she felt perversely pleased at the flicker of irritation which crossed his face. He turned away. 'Bridget, how are you?' he asked, calmly ignoring the highly charged atmosphere. He kissed the older woman's cheek and greeted Frank with some comment which made him laugh.

Leigh felt a tug at her sleeve.

'Hello, I'm Benjy.'

'I know you are,' she smiled, grateful for a release from the almost unbearable awareness of Jake.

'I remember you.' His voice was solemn as he squinted up through a fall of heavy black hair.

'That's very clever. The last time I saw you, you were only a tiny boy. You must have an excellent memory.'

He took hold of her hand, dragging her to the sofa where he plopped himself down beside her, his thin legs sticking out rigidly before him. 'Daddy said you were a foxy lady, but you don't look like a fox to me.' He screwed up his nose in puzzlement. 'I think you're nice.'

'Thank you.' Leigh studiously ignored the reference to Jake. 'How do you like school?'

'It's great. I'm in Mrs White's class.'

Frank came over and sat down beside them, ruffling Benjy's hair. 'How's the sailing going, young man?'

Benjy beamed and puffed out his small chest. 'I'm doing well, aren't I, Daddy?' Jake nodded his agreement from across the room where he was chatting to Bridget. 'Daddy's teaching me. He hires a little dinghy and takes me out every Saturday. I can capsize now.'

'Has he made you the captain yet?' Frank asked.

The boy stuck out his lower lip, 'Not yet. I'm just the crew.' He sighed loudly and everyone laughed. Jake and Bridget had finished their conversation and turned to look at him. 'I can water-ski, too,' Benjy added, basking in the undivided attention of the four adults. 'Well, not properly,' he admitted with a cautious glance at his father, 'but I can stay up for almost a minute.'

'Thirty seconds if the gods are with you,' Jake said drily, 'but you're improving.' He turned to Frank. 'You must have a day out with us on the speedboat some time.'

'That would be lovely,' Bridget pounced on the suggestion like a child on a Christmas present. 'Perhaps we could do that while Leigh's over. You'd love that, wouldn't you, darlin'?' She put her hand on Jake's arm. 'She's like a mermaid in the water. You should see her in the pool, she swims like a fish!'

Leigh flushed. 'A cod,' she said flatly.

'Better than a shark,' Jake's brows lifted a fraction. 'Especially a man-eating one. Shall we go now?' He turned to Bridget. 'If you would excuse us.'

'Can I sit on the peacock chair, Aunt Bridget? Just for a minute,' Benjy pleaded. Bridget cast a swift questioning look at Jake. He nodded. Everyone watched as Benjy climbed on to the high seat of the imposing chair. He folded his arms regally and stared haughtily into space.

'Fantasy time,' grinned Jake. 'Now we must leave. It's way past his bedtime, but he was so keen to visit Aunt Bridget I hadn't the heart to refuse.' Bridget smiled her pleasure at the compliment. 'I promise I'll deliver this mermaid home at a decent hour before she turns into a cod.' Jake raised two mocking eyebrows, which made Benjy abandon his pose and giggle.

Jake's dark green Mercedes was waiting in the car park.

'It was good of Sunantha to take the time to telephone me,' Leigh said with asperity as she slid into the front seat of the car beside him.

'Don't get on your high horse,' he replied calmly. 'I

was about to telephone you myself, but some important customers arrived unexpectedly. I apologise. I didn't want to leave the invitation until too late in the day in case Bridget had rounded up another suitor for you, so I asked Sunantha to do the honours.'

She digested his explanation, then turned to him. 'Are we dining alone?'

'Why? Are you afraid?' he taunted. 'You don't want Bridget and Frank along to hold your hand, do you? Surely you're a big girl now?' He cast a quick glance over his shoulder at Benjy, who was kneeling on the back seat, and lowered his voice. 'If you have any doubts about your safety, please dismiss them. I promise I'll be a paragon of virtue.' His eyes flashed with amusement. 'I have no intention of outraging your modesty, as the newspapers call it here.'

She flushed. 'I didn't expect you would. I merely wondered if Choo would be dining with us.'

'She's having the evening off. It gives her a break, and she wants to take the baby over to see some friends.' He thrust the car into gear with a powerful fist. 'I hope you're prepared to consider a second try at peaceful co-existence. We got off to a bad start in the lift. The atmosphere shouldn't be so fraught with tension second time around.'

'What's "atmosphere", Daddy?' Benjy leaned forward, a small elbow on the back of each of their seats.

'Little pitchers have big ears,' Jake commented drily, and Leigh averted her head, leaving him to struggle singlehandedly with a definition of the word 'atmosphere' to satisfy a five-year-old.

It was only a ten-minute drive from the apartment to his large Old Colonial style house on the most expensive piece of real estate on the island. Leigh was conscious of the faint aroma of his musky aftershave in her nostrils and the hard stretch of his long legs beside hers. Benjy chattered away happily, requiring only brief comments from his father, so she was able to study Jake, sneaking covert glances at him as he concentrated on the road. As she had surmised he was well dressed in stylish tailored navy slacks and a matching silk shirt with his initials monogrammed discreetly on the pocket. A heavy chrome Rolex watch glinted on his broad wrist as he swung the steering wheel. The evening traffic was heavy, as usual, and he accelerated briskly, the powerful car surging forward to overtake a slow moving truck on the left. Smoothly he veered to the other side of the road to pass a hesitant taxi. Leigh's eyes opened wide. She had forgotten just how precarious driving in Singapore could be. He glanced at her profile.

'I drive like I sail, to suit the prevailing conditions. Amazingly, when I return to Britain I slip back into being a courteous driver again, but here I interpret the Highway Code to suit myself.'

'Like everyone else!' Leigh added.

He gave a chuckle and effortlessly swung the car into the driveway of a large white house. They parked beneath a covered porch crowded with bougainvilleas, crotons and mother-in-law's tongue in vast red pots.

'Remember the gekkos?' He pointed to the ceiling of the porch where a family of small grey house lizards hung motionless. Suddenly one darted forward to catch an alien fly on its tongue. A swift gulp and the fly was gone. Yellow light from the house gleamed through the openwork carving on the front door. Benjy tumbled from the car and waited impatiently as Jake fitted his key into the lock.

'Welcome,' he grinned as Leigh stepped before him into the parquet-floored hall. The ground floor of the house was open plan, dominated by a spacious, high-ceilinged living room, one side of which was entirely open to the garden. A Spanish style black wrought iron screen pulled across at night for security.

'It's just as I remembered it,' she commented, looking around.

'I wish I spent more time at home.' He gave a sigh. 'I'm almost a stranger here. The house is Choo's domain.'

As her eyes rested on the plump settees and highly polished furniture Leigh wondered why nothing of Choo's personality was reflected in the room. True enough, fresh flower arrangements of golden and bronze chrysanthemums stood on side tables, but there was no lived in feeling, no spontaneity. The room was too formal. It looked like a photograph in an upmarket homes and gardens magazine. It was colour co-ordinated, almost excessively so, in muted shades of beige, gold and brown, but it lacked a personal touch. Everything had been purchased at a price, but there was no love. No needlework cushions worked by a caring hand, no collections of coral, not even an errant box of building cubes which Benjy might have left around. She remembered the comfortable feel of the apartment she and Patrick had shared, the miscellany of straw hats she had pinned to the kitchen wall, the shells they had gathered together, the pieces of blue and white pottery discovered in Thieves' Market.

'Smell the frangipani,' Jake ordered as they walked across to look out into the garden. The fragrance was sweet and heady. The garden was full of blossoms, glowing beneath discreetly arranged spotlights. A colourful Yellow Flame tree stood in the centre of the lawn, while a mass of orange and cyclamen bougainvilleas tumbled in profusion over a wooden trellis in the distance. To one side was a square patio.

Benjy threw himself down on to a plump beige velvet floor cushion which was one of three carefully arranged on a corner of the shaggy carpet.

'Don't bother making yourself comfortable, young man,' Jake said with mock ferocity. 'Say goodnight—it's bedtime.'

The small boy pulled a face but rose reluctantly to his feet. He smiled at Leigh, then catapulted forward, his thin arms clinging around her waist. She bent down and his soft mouth hit hers in a sudden kiss. 'I like you,' he whispered.

'I like you, too.'

'*Bed*,' Jake repeated firmly, and Benjy hurtled from the room. 'Don't forget to clean your teeth,' Jake shouted after him. 'I'll be along to tuck you up in a minute.'

The eagerness of Benjy's embrace touched Leigh's heart. 'Does he miss not having a mother?' she asked before she could stop herself, although well aware it was the kind of personal question Jake would dislike.

'He has Choo.' The severity of his expression warned her not to probe further. 'Can I give you a drink?' The sudden tautness was pushed aside to reveal the charming host. 'Or has Bridget warned you against the dangers of men plying you with alcohol?'

'I don't need her to tell me what I should or shouldn't do,' she replied tartly. 'I'll have a vodka and Coke, please.'

Jake pulled a face and for a second looked the same age as his son. 'That sounds disgusting! Are you sure you really like it, or are you trying to impress me?'

'Why should I bother to impress you?' she gave a saccharine-sweet smile. 'I like it and I want it—please.' There was a bite of temper hidden in her reply which made him eye her warily. Then he shrugged one wide shoulder and picked up a glass from a small bar in the corner of the room.

'I'll slum it with a plain gin and tonic,' he commented with a derisive curl of his lip, handing her the glass. 'We're eating on the patio, it's cooler out there. Choo set the table and prepared the food before she left. I'll fetch everything from the kitchen later.'

'Does Choo have many friends in Singapore?' Leigh asked.

He took a swig from his drink before answering. 'To be honest I don't really know, but she had a phone call this evening which seemed to make her very happy. She went off in a great rush, the baby straddling her hip as usual.'

'You're not often at home on a weekday, are you?' Leigh ran a fingertip around the rim of her glass.

'Not often. All this travelling is proving to be a problem. As Benjy gets older he needs me more.' He frowned. 'Still, doubtless I shall be leaving Milwain International before too long.'

Leigh stared at him in amazement. 'But it's your life!' she burst out.

'Maybe, but there's no way I shall stay around to work for young Rory.' The cold fury in his voice surprised her.

His feelings of resentment obviously ran deep.

'But he'd be in London and you'd be here, surely you could function as you do now?'

'You think he'd allow that?' he sneered. 'I have no illusions. He'll get rid of me as soon as he can. He'll force me out once he's in control.' He took another gulp of the gin. 'Still, as far as Benjy is concerned I'd probably be better off in a nine-to-five job. I worry myself sick about him when I'm away, wondering if he's all right. Poor little devil, he doesn't know what a proper family life is like. I feel so guilty about him missing out. I thought things would be easier as he grew older, but they get worse.' Jake ran his fingers through his thick hair. 'I'm sorry, I didn't invite you here so I could pour out my troubles, true confessions are not usually my style.'

'That's true.'

He cast her a thoughtful look, then grinned. 'How did you enjoy your prearranged dinner date last night?'

'It wasn't prearranged,' she retaliated. 'Rory asked me out of his own accord.'

'Come on, Leigh,' he teased. 'You should have heard Bridget extolling your virtues—she made you sound like a cross between Joan of Arc and Raquel Welch, if that's possible! The poor fellow had no choice.'

'Nonsense! He could have ignored me.'

'With Bridget breathing down his neck? You'd have to have a will of iron to avoid her scheming.'

'You appear to have succeeded,' she retorted.

'I *have* a will of iron,' he said smugly, rising to his feet. 'If you'll excuse me for a few minutes I'll go and see if that young scamp of mine is in his bed.' He strode purposefully from the room, leaving Leigh to sink back against the soft cushions. A conversation with Jake was like a trek through a minefield, you never knew when something was going to blow up in your face. But the maddening aspect was that she knew he deliberately baited her and enjoyed doing so, yet each time she rose to the attack. The cooler Jake appeared, the more tetchy she became, which was out of character; she wasn't usually so volatile, only in his company.

CHAPTER FOUR

LEIGH gave a deep sigh and sipped her drink. She had needed Jake's coolness at one time in her life. When Patrick had been killed he had taken charge and she had drawn on his emotional strength, for she had been in no fit state to do anything else. He had attended to her needs, competently providing every possible assistance. His visits had been frequent, making her aware of what was happening, penetrating the nightmare world which surrounded her. For once his business had been abandoned in order that he could look after her. Efficiently he had coped with the welter of necessary arrangements, sending air tickets to Patrick's parents in order that they might attend the funeral, acknowledging the flood of sympathetic letters. He had stood by her side at the morgue when she had said a tearful farewell to her young husband, putting his strong arms around her as she swayed, overcome by the tragic sight of Patrick's broken body.

She knew she should have been grateful for his compassion, but she had drifted distractedly through the painful days, hardly aware of his presence. She had taken his support entirely for granted, accepting his efforts as no more than her right. Jake expected no appreciation, which was just as well, for from Leigh he had received only a few half-hearted gestures of thanks. She had no energy to give more. Later the initial haze of despair began to clear, and with a cold, cruel clarity she knew only hatred—hatred of Jake.

Patrick was still tired and pale when the assignment in Kuantan on the east coast of Malaysia had cropped up. 'I'll take the car,' he had planned as they lay languidly in bed one Sunday morning. 'It's a five-hour drive, but the simplest way. If I fly to Kuala Lumpur and motor across country it will take forever, and I don't want to be away from home any longer than is necessary. I can be there and back in a day.' He had reached across and stroked Leigh's bare shoulder. 'I'd much rather be here with you than sleeping alone in some dreary hotel.' He put his arm around her, pulling her close, his lips in her hair, and she knew he wanted her.

She pulled away. 'Wouldn't it be wiser to stay somewhere overnight?' she fretted. 'Ten hours' driving is too much—you'll be exhausted!'

'Don't fuss,' he had murmured, his fingers sliding over the smooth skin of her throat down to the fullness of her breasts. 'I promise if I feel tired I'll find a hotel and stop for the night, but if the meeting finishes early I'll motor back home—very slowly.' He put a hand over her lips to silence her protests. 'Okay?' he insisted quietly. 'Now shut up. I want to make love to you.' His mouth had become insistent and her fears were swept away on a tide of mounting passion.

She had waited up until midnight on the Monday evening, listening to records and reading, but Patrick didn't arrive home. With some relief she realised he must have broken his journey and spent the night at a hotel in Malaysia. He would, no doubt, arrive back around noon the next day. Leigh went to bed consoled by the knowledge that he was being sensible. She slept deeply, which was fortunate, it was to be her last good night's sleep for many months.

The next morning she had climbed out of bed refreshed and pulled on a baby pink towelling robe before padding into the kitchen. She plugged in the percolator and looked out of the window at the city which stretched below like a well tended garden, green and clean. A light breeze stirred fronds of the Majestic palms which surrounded the apartment block. Happily she hummed to herself as she cut a slice of pale orange papaya, topping it with a lemon wedge. The aroma of freshly perked coffee filled the air, and she sniffed appreciatively. The day promised to be a busy one. A game of squash was fixed with a girl friend for eleven, and there was a Chinese brush painting class later. The doorbell rang as she was retrieving toast from the grill. The thought flashed hopefully through her mind that, somehow, perhaps Patrick had come home. She tucked a strand of auburn hair behind her ear as she opened the door. Jake stood there, and as soon as she saw his face, taut and grim, she knew something was wrong.

'What's the matter?' she asked weakly, her legs turning to jelly.

He strode forward, closing the door behind him and shepherding her into the living room. 'Sit down,' he said gently. She perched on the arm of the sofa, her large blue eyes looking up at him in bewilderment. She looks like an angel in that soft pink robe, Jake thought viciously, so young and innocent. Her thick hair curled around her face, and he longed to take her in his arms and protect her from the harsh realities of the world.

'It's Patrick, isn't it?' she asked, her voice faltering. Without speaking he nodded his head. His eyes were bright. He rubbed at his forehead savagely, fighting to control his emotions. 'I'm very, very sorry, but Patrick's had an accident in the car.' He hesitated, gripping his hands together until the blood drained from his knuckles.

Leigh felt herself grow cold. 'Is he dead?' she demanded wildly.

'Yes.' His voice was low.

'Dead?' she repeated, shaking her head in disbelief. 'But he was coming home this morning?'

'I know.' Jake pushed her gently down on to the sofa and knelt beside her, taking hold of her limp, unresisting hand. The stunned look in her eyes almost crucified him. 'It happened in the early hours of this morning. He motored back from Kuantan in the dark, after the meeting. It must have finished very late. He entered Singapore around two a.m. The accident happened a couple of miles south of the checkpoint on a stretch of dual carriageway. His car left the road and crashed into a tree and he was killed outright. He didn't suffer.' Jake's fingers urgently smoothed the back of her hand in a vain attempt to calm her. She looked frantically around the room as though seeking reassurance from another source.

'It's a mistake, a horrible mistake,' she whimpered blindly. 'Patrick can't be dead. My Patrick! I love him.' Her eyes lit upon a photograph of them both on the desk. They had been swimming and a friend had snapped them, young and laughing and in love, their arms around each other. Her chest heaved and she had begun to sob, harsh, brittle sobs which almost broke Jake's heart in two.

Her in-laws had arrived from England and after her first tearful meeting with them she had cried no more in their presence. Her unnatural calmness and rigid self-control made them deeply concerned, but she steadfastly refused to discuss Patrick's death, turning her face away from the real world. Instead she retreated into herself, blocking out other people, their sorrow and their sympathy. Three days later her young husband had been cremated and his ashes scattered on alien soil. She had glided, wraithlike, through the service as though she were in another world herself, a mere ghost automatically attending to the rituals of life. She was protected by an enveloping numbness. This nightmare was happening to someone else, a composed, pale-faced young widow in black. Soon she would awaken and Patrick would be there. His arms would reach out for her, and there would be love shining in his eyes.

But she was unable to delude herself for long. The blessed numbness began to fade and raw pain intruded. She fought to remain impassive during the day when other people were around, but at night, in the darkness of her room, she succumbed to the almost unbearable weight of her grief. She sobbed into her pillow, hoping to obliterate the sound, for Patrick's parents had insisted they stay on for a few days after the funeral. In the morning her eyes were red and wild with weeping, and she was exhausted. Her in-laws exchanged worried looks, and Leigh was relieved when they left and she could be alone.

'You must come and live with us,' Bridget had insisted over the telephone. 'I don't like to think of you all alone. Frank and I would love to look after you. You know you can treat our home as your own. Are you sure you're getting enough to eat?'

'I'm sure.' If only Bridget knew how food nauseated her! She was existing on cups of coffee. 'Thank you for the invitation, but I'm perfectly all right here. I don't want to leave my own home.'

'Suppose I come and sleep at the apartment with you? Then you won't be lonely.'

'No, thank you. I shall only be here for a few more days until the packers arrive, and then I'm flying back home.'

'I'll come and keep you company during the day,' Bridget offered.

'No!' Leigh's voice cut through the conversation with the finality of a blade, and Bridget was forced to retreat.

Leigh's real reason for remaining in her Singapore home after the funeral was a deeply emotional one. If she had wished she could have easily flown home with her parents-in-law, Jake would have organised the shipment of her possessions. But she could not tear herself away from Patrick's memory. While she remained on the island her thoughts of him were vivid. She lay in bed at night and pretended he was still alive. She could stretch out her hand in the darkness and imagine the feel of him. Leigh was terrified that when she flew away, over the oceans and continents, she would be flying away from him, too. All she had left were memories, and she was haunted with the fear that they would become fainter with each mile as she retreated half a world away.

It was as she lay alone, distraught, in the still empty hours of the night that she began to realise the role Jake had played in her misery. He had known of Patrick's ill-health and yet had insisted he fulfil the assignment in Kuantan. Jake was well aware of the distances, the exhausting hours in the car, but, as usual, he had put the company first and had ruthlessly ordered Patrick to go. A bud of unreasonable hatred began to swell inside her. Jake was Patrick's murderer as surely as if he had pulled out a gun and shot him.

The packers arrived and stripped the apartment clean. When they left Leigh wandered around, dragging her fingers disconsolately across the empty shelves, the deserted desk. All her belongings were packed in padded cartons for the long sea journey back to England, only the impersonal company furniture remained. Tomorrow she would leave the island. Her suitcase lay half packed in the bedroom. Tonight would be the last time she would lie in the bed where she and Patrick had made such overwhelming love. She sat down, head in her hands, her long hair tumbling over her shoulders. As she closed her eyes the sweet torment of her memories began.

'Are you all right?' A deep voice broke the silence. Jake stood in the doorway, looking anxiously across at her, his eyes sweeping over the barren apartment and the melancholy attitude of the girl. 'Get your suitcase,' he said firmly. 'You're not staying here alone tonight. I know you've resisted all Bridget's efforts and I understand. She'd drive you mad with her incessant chatter, but you must come and stay with me this evening. I'm not leaving you here all by yourself. My aunt will be delighted to see you, and she'll respect your need for privacy.'

Leigh raised her head and glared at him, her eyes sparking with anger. 'Get out and leave me alone!' she snapped.

'What do you mean?' He walked towards her, hurt and puzzlement on his face.

'I wouldn't stay under your roof if you were the last person on earth,' she spat out, 'Patrick's death is your responsibility, yours alone, Jake. You killed him! All you care about is making money for that damn company. You brought him out to Singapore in the first place because you knew he was a hard worker, and, my word, you've certainly had your money's worth!' Her harsh laugh was ugly. 'He was a sick man. He'd worked himself into the ground. You knew he hadn't recovered fully from the virus, and yet you forced him to drive up to Kuantan. I hate you,' her voice rose hysterically, thin and shrill. 'I hate you, Jake St John! You killed my husband!' Then her eyes had been blinded with tears and she had turned savagely away. Her arms were rigid by her sides, her fists clenched as she tried to overcome the deep sobs that racked her body. She heard Jake move behind her and felt his hand on her shoulder. She shook it away violently.

'It wasn't like that at all. You can't really mean it. You don't know what you're saying,' he implored.

She had turned to him, taking vicious pleasure at the pain in his eyes. Then a strange, angry calm filled her. The trembling of her body ceased and she curled her lip at his plea. 'Yes, I do,' her voice was glacial. 'Oh yes, I do. Now get out and leave me alone.' She saw the naked distress on his face. Let him suffer, she thought with loathing, let him lie awake at nights, like me.

Jake had left the apartment immediately, his face grim. He knew Leigh was in a state of shock, but to accuse him of sending Patrick to his death was totally unjust. Patrick had been his friend. They had worked so well together, delighting in orders they won, commiserating over failed chances. Why should she consider Patrick's death was his fault? True, he was the head of the company and supervised the overall organisation, but they had worked as a team. He had never expected more of Patrick than he would expect of himself. Jake had tossed and turned all night, reliving the accusation time and time again, and the next morning found him pacing the floor of his office as he tried to decide what to do. He couldn't allow Leigh to leave with such a twisted view of events. He came to a decision: he would go and see her again and try to set the record straight. Sunantha watched in amazement as her usually calm employer strode out, running his fingers worriedly through his hair and mumbling incoherently about returning later.

After parking his car in the grounds of the apartment Jake sat for several minutes, his hands gripping the wheel as he decided how to approach her. He was desperate for Leigh to understand the true situation, and hoped that after a night's rest she would be calmer and realise the inaccuracy of her dramatic accusation. He knew she had been worried about Patrick's health, that was only natural, but she had always seemed so reasonable in the past. Surely, by now, she would have seen sense, but when he had rung the bell she had faced him like a hostile stranger.

'I must talk to you before you leave this evening,' he had said. 'Can I come in?'

'No.' Her face was rigid with distaste. 'If you have something to say, say it here on the doorstep.'

'You're being a bitch, a cold-blooded little bitch,' he said fiercely, the hard pain inside him growing into anger at the sight of such illogical hatred. 'I realise you're shocked, but don't you give a damn how anyone else feels?'

'I suppose by anyone else you mean yourself?' She raised her chin defiantly.

'Yes, I do,' he replied harshly. 'Don't you think I'm devastated by Patrick's death too? We had a great relationship. I miss him now. I shall miss him in the future.' Jake had laid his head wearily against the door frame. There was darkness around his eyes, and his mouth was taut. 'You're not making things any easier, acting like this. You *can't* blame me. What you're saying is blatantly untrue.'

'I do blame you.' Leigh's gaze was steady and there was more than a hint of cruelty in the glitter of her narrowed eyes. 'It's perfectly clear to me that all you really care about is self-glorification, and you achieve that by making sure the company breaks all records. Jake St John, super-successful business executive, Tuan Number One,' she sneered. 'But what about Patrick's contribution? You worked him to death. You used his efforts to turn in bigger and better profits.'

'Patrick came to Singapore of his own free will,' he explained desperately. 'He wasn't a child. He was ambitious. He was in a responsible position for which he earned a high salary. You were both delighted with the move, remember? He was unfortunate enough to catch a virus, and I know he was tired, but that happens to many businessmen out here. The rewards are high in the East, but you have to work for them. Heaven knows, nobody travels more than I.' A nerve twitched in his cheek. 'And don't forget Patrick played hard, too. He made little effort to recuperate when he was at home. He enjoyed parties. You were both always rushing off somewhere. He made no attempt to pace himself, he wanted to live life to the full. He was going through a bad patch, healthwise, but it would have cleared in time.'

'And what about the Kuantan visit?' she asked bitterly.

'That was routine. Patrick made his own decisions. I didn't supervise his every movement. His death was an accident. Anything could have happened. Perhaps he swerved to avoid a stray dog on the road, or nodded off to sleep for a brief moment.' Jake lifted his hands, then dropped them down to his side. 'I don't know, but I do know you're wrong to blame me.'

Leigh glared at him. He was so sure of his convictions. 'Perhaps that's your opinion, but it isn't mine,' she snapped relentlessly. 'I know exactly who was responsible for my husband's death.' Abruptly she stepped back into the room and slammed the door in Jake's face before noisily pushing the bolt across. He rang the bell again and again, but there was no reply from within, and eventually he retraced his steps to the office.

Leigh had not seen him again before she left for England. Bridget and Frank had driven her to the airport and she had told them nothing of her feelings. She boarded the plane, and among the stale mixture of half formed emotions was a feeling of relief. She was escaping from Jake's influence, from the man she hated.

It soon became apparent from Bridget's letters that he had chosen to remain silent about her accusation, and she let the matter rest. Over the following months her hatred had diminished, its bright, obsessive flame burning out to leave ashes of disquiet. She began to accept Patrick's death as an act of fate. It was too easy to blame only Jake. She recognised that other factors had played a part, and yet she still believed that Jake had been the catalyst for the tragedy. As time passed the thought had been hidden away, and his involvement no longer seemed important. Nothing could alter the facts. The time for recrimination was long gone. Leigh sighed. It was only since her return to Singapore that her memories had been brought into sharper focus. She had no wish to stir up the bitter feelings of the past, but couldn't put aside an uneasy awareness of unfinished business.

'At last, one child put to bed,' Jake's deep voice interrupted her thoughts. 'Sorry I took so long. Benjy is rapidly becoming a pain in the neck at bedtimes. I've told Choo to stand no nonsense, but he wraps her around his little finger, then expects to do the same with me!' He bent down to pick up his glass. 'Every night he finds some excuse to delay the final farewell. Just now we had a long discussion over whether or not you should be called up to kiss him goodnight.'

'I would have liked that,' said Leigh.

He gulped down the dregs of his drink. 'I know you would, and thanks, but I'd rather he sticks to a routine. Bridget's always taking him out and spoiling him, but it's dangerous, I don't want him to become too dependent on her kindness. What he's never had, he'll never miss.'

'That's very harsh,' Leigh scolded. 'Don't be too severe. He's little more than a baby, he needs affection. You make it sound as though a few hugs and kisses are anathema!'

He tugged thoughtfully at the lobe of his ear. 'Hardly. But I'm wary of him becoming too attached to anyone, especially as we'll soon be on the move. You can't imagine the trauma he went through when my aunt left. He was heartbroken. His sad little face haunted me night and day. I swore I'd protect him from that kind of distress again.'

'So you protect him from love!'

'No,' he said impatiently, 'he has me.'

'And Choo.'

'That's different.'

She waited for some kind of explanation, but none was forthcoming. It suddenly struck her that Jake was protecting Benjy from pain in the same way she was protecting herself—by holding back. She frowned. It wasn't an ideal solution to either her, or Benjy's, problems, but what alternative was there? Both of them had suffered by loving too much. And Jake too, she realised, must have gone through the same torture when his wife had died. No, Leigh decided, it was dangerous to care too much. She'd been head over heels in love with Patrick, and look what had happened—fate had snatched him away. She couldn't afford to take that risk again.

She looked up as Jake retrieved the two empty glasses and walked towards the kitchen door. 'If you'd give me a hand in carrying the food out to the patio, we can start dinner. Choo couldn't leave everything out earlier, the ants would have gobbled it up before we did.' He held open the swing door into the kitchen, and as Leigh passed close to him she was tantalisingly aware of the hard maleness of his body.

Everything was prepared. A savoury flan was on a low light in the oven, while a tossed salad was crisply waiting in the fridge. Jake loaded them both up with dishes and ushered her before him on to the patio. The soft glow of wall lights revealed that a rattan suite in green and white cotton had been pushed aside, leaving a wide area where a table had been carefully set for two.

'Choo must imagine we're lovers,' he commented with a half smile, gazing down at the white damask cloth and heavy silver, and Leigh's heart lurched irrationally at his words. 'I don't receive this kind of treatment when I eat with my son.' The table was exquisitely set. Crystal wine and water glasses sparkled in the light and a shining silver candelabrum holding two deep purple candles stood to one side of the place settings. A circular posy of violet orchids graced the centre of the table, and there were napkins of lavender linen.

'It looks lovely,' she agreed. The setting was certainly romantic. The covered patio jutted out from the body of the house, overlooking the darkened garden on three sides. It was difficult to ascertain where the patio ended and lawns began, for huge glazed pots bearing lavish flowering shrubs surrounded the perimeter of the white marble floor. The air was warm, with the caress of a soft breeze, and stars twinkled high above in the night sky. Silver and black shadows moved and faded in the garden. Jake lit the candles. A smile lurked at the corner of his mouth, indicating his amusement at Choo's obvious attempt at a romantic dinner for two. It seemed odd that she should make such an effort for Jake and another woman, Leigh mused idly, but Choo's was an Asian mind, and as such was probably beyond her comprehension.

The meal was delicious. Whatever inadequacies Choo appeared to have in stamping her individual mark on the house, they did not spill over into her cooking. Jake had chosen a dry white wine, and after the main course produced a rich chocolate mousse. He was a witty and attentive host, and despite her reservations Leigh found herself responding to his easy charm. The conversation flowed naturally, as though they were old friends, which, on the surface, they were, but throughout it all was an undercurrent—a silver thread of tantalising danger, a tenuous strand of excitement, challenge, love, lust—Leigh couldn't decide which, but it couldn't be ignored. She wondered if he intended to kiss her. Common sense decreed it would be better if their relationship was a formal one, but perversely she knew she would be faintly disappointed if he was content to keep the evening on a purely platonic level, though she didn't know why.

'Okay if I smoke?' he enquired.

'Go ahead.' She watched as he lit a cigar from the brilliant flame of a heavy gold lighter. He inhaled deeply, and a whisper of grey smoke drifted across, filling her nostrils with the aromatic, altogether male smell of an expensive cigar.

'We'll have coffee in the living room,' he decided, pushing back his chair.

'Can I help with the dishes?'

'No, thanks. I'll just take the plates back to the kitchen to escape the ants. Choo will deal with everything in the morning.'

They walked through into the large room. Leigh sat down on a comfortable sofa and fingered the slender gold chain at her neck. The wine, and Jake's company, had combined to produce a contented, mellow glow. She smiled to herself. Within minutes he was back, bearing the coffee tray with white bone china cups and saucers on a spotless cloth, and a tiny spray of deep purple orchids.

'She never stops trying!' Jake commented with a smile, noticing Leigh's sidelong glance at the flowers. He placed the tray on a long, low table before the sofa. 'Brandy?' he asked, standing over her, his hair falling forward across his brow.

'Please, just a small one.'

'You're being completely reckless this evening,' he teased. 'First wine, and now brandy, not forgetting that disgusting concoction you downed at the outset.' He poured a little brandy into two crystal goblets and handed one to her. Leigh smiled her thanks. Jake sat down close beside her, his eyes soft and serious. Leigh was conscious of his look and glanced down in confusion at the amber liquid in the glass in her hands, her heart slipping and sliding all over the place. Slowly she took a sip, and the brandy coursed down her throat like a stream of liquid fire. Jake set his goblet down on the low table, and stretched his arm along the back of the sofa behind her. The twang of a tuk-tuk bird in distant trees broke the silence. Leigh took another sip of brandy, and tried, desperately, to find some bright comment with which to shatter her tense awareness of him. Then she felt the cool touch of his fingers at the nape of her neck. Slowly, insistently he stroked the smooth skin, arousing her, setting her blood flowing hotly in her veins. A warning bell rang in her ears, but when she turned her head the desire in his eyes made her bones melt and the bell was silenced.

Jake bent his head to hers. His kiss was hungry, setting her aflame. He paused to remove the glass from her quivering grasp, then his mouth came down on hers again, potent and possessive. His kisses covered her face, her hair, her throat, and Leigh was lost in the grip of overpowering desire. Instinctively she slid an arm around his neck and he pulled her closer until she could feel the muscular stretch of his body against hers.

'I want you so much,' Jake murmured unsteadily into her hair, as his hands caressed her, making her nerve ends burn with delight. Tenderly he trailed long fingers across her face, tracing the outline of her cheekbones and jaw. As he touched her mouth she parted her lips, briefly catching his fingers in sharp white teeth. He kissed her again, his mouth bruising hers with the savage passion of his embrace. His hands slid beneath her jacket and across the naked skin of her shoulders, and she moved restlessly. The desire which had been denied for two sterile, empty years throbbed desperately within her. For too long she had deluded herself that she had no need of masculine love. Now the pretence was shattered and she gave herself up willingly into his arms. Jake removed her jacket and pushed aside the thin fabric of her dress. 'No bra?' he whispered with amusement into her ear.

'I'm a liberated woman,' she replied, running her hands through his thick hair, twisting it around her fingers, capturing him. He stroked the silky skin, feeling the dark nipples pucker beneath his touch. Her desire deepened with his.

'My beautiful girl,' he groaned huskily. Leigh slipped her fingers beneath his shirt, feeling the crisp hair on his strong chest. His muscles contracted at the caress of her touch and she felt the pounding of his heart. He lowered his head, kissing her throat, the valley between her breasts. Gently, sensually, he ran his tongue around her hard nipples, and she shuddered, arching her back, thrusting herself forward, desperate for the feel of the hard length of his body against hers. She moaned softly as his kisses roused her to an almost unbearable pitch where coherent thought had vanished, leaving behind only sensation—such wonderful sensation. Jake's breathing was hard and quick and his touch increased in urgency as his hands explored her body. Suddenly he stiffened and raised his head from her burning skin. Leigh was vaguely conscious of a child crying, far away.

'Daddy!' Benjy was calling from his room. Jake sighed, his lips returning insistently to caress her trembling body. Leigh stirred as Benjy cried out again.

'Oh no!' The frustration was thick in his voice. His lips moved along the curve of her throat and on to her mouth. 'Perhaps he'll go back to sleep,' he muttered hopefully, his hands unable to relinquish the compelling contours of her body.

'Daddy, Daddy!' the cries came again, louder.

He sighed in despair. 'What a time to want a drink of water, or whatever,' he complained. He kissed her lingeringly, unable to release her.

Leigh moved, pushing him away gently. 'You'd better go and see what he wants,' she said, smiling at the reluctance in his eyes.

With an effort he sat back and ran his hand through his tousled hair. 'I'm sorry about this, my love. I'll murder that devil son of mine! I'll be as quick as I can.' He smiled at her, then, tucking his tumbled shirt back into his trousers, he left the room.

Leigh sank back. Her heart thumped a wild music which sang in her ears. She was weak with desire, her emotions in uproar. Her face was flushed and her skin glowed from the urgent touch of Jake's hands. She breathed deeply, trying to control the impetuous rise and fall of her chest. With shaking fingers she pulled up her dress and replaced the jacket, then she repinned the heavy bun at the back of her head, tucking in the loose tendrils of hair which Jake had loosened in his onslaught. She must look respectable, just in case Benjy appeared, though she suspected Jake would deal firmly with his errant son and quickly return. He was a passionate lover and the desire in his eyes indicated that he needed, and expected, fulfilment.

The minutes ticked by. Leigh glanced at her watch; it was almost eleven-thirty. She leant forward and poured out a cup of coffee, still hot from the flask. Gradually her breathing quietened and she became calmer, the pulsating beat within slackened and the kaleidoscope of whirling emotions settled. She began to wonder where all her good resolutions had disappeared to. She had intended to keep cool and calm in Jake's presence, out of harm's way, but instead she had fallen into his arms. So readily. Her face flamed as she remembered how eager she had been for his kisses. Leigh chewed at her lower lip. What a fool she had been! She had offered not the slightest resistance, instead the demands of her body had swept her away. How willingly she had been seduced!

Leigh drank the hot coffee rapidly. How could she have been so naïve! After all, she was well aware of Jake's reputation, and now she was just another female to add to his list. She had imagined she was on her guard, but it had taken only the touch of his fingers to disarm her. She laughed tersely. How could she have wanted his kisses and the feel of his arms around her after all he had done to wreck her life? With clenched teeth she decided that there was no point denying the yearning need which he had aroused, but surely that was merely a result of being deprived of love for so long? It was only natural she should respond to a masculine touch, especially when the man was as experienced as Jake. She and Patrick had enjoyed a vigorous love life, and she missed him, even now. Many, many nights she had lain alone in her bed, yearning for his virile, muscular body. But it had only been Patrick she had ever desired; she had scorned the touch of any other man. Jake had caught her in a weak moment when the wine had made her soft and foolishly agreeable. He had awakened dormant desires which she considered no longer existed, but she hadn't really wanted *him* at all; it was his dominant masculinity which had carried her

away. Her senses had reeled at the hard strength of his
arms, the rough rub of his chin, the overwhelming
maleness of him.

He must have realised she would be vulnerable after
two years alone and that her defence would be shaky.
No doubt he had planned his seduction and she, being
unbelievably stupid, had fallen like a ripe fruit into his
hands.

She sat up, straightening her shoulders. It must be
made perfectly clear to him that her behaviour this
evening had been a mistake. She wasn't the kind of girl
who entered into casual affairs, indeed she had been a
virgin when she had married Patrick, and she saw no
reason now to abandon her principles. She had told Jake
she was a liberated woman, but her liberation did not
extend to promiscuous sex. If other girls leapt in and
out of bed willy-nilly, then that was their concern, but
she did not intend to follow suit. Men seemed to imagine
that because she was a young and pretty widow her
morals were flexible, but that was not so.

Leigh heard his footsteps on the stairs and stood up
briskly. Her mouth was suddenly dry with apprehension,
and there were butterflies in her stomach. Obviously he
would be angry, she didn't blame him, but she must try
to make him understand her point of view.

'Benjy's fine now.' Jake came to her side. 'He had a
bad dream, but it was soon forgotten and he's fallen
asleep again.' As he reached for her she moved, rebuff-
ing the soft look of love in his eyes.

'What's the matter?' he asked, instantly sensing her
change of mood.

'I think I'd better leave. It's almost midnight,' she
said quickly, stepping backwards and forcing him to
release her arms.

He rubbed a finger roughly against his temple in agitation. 'What do you mean?' He was perplexed. 'It won't
matter if you're late. Bridget gave you a key. You can't
leave me now.' He looked down at her, a question in his
eyes, then he put his hands firmly on her shoulders and
drew her towards him. His lips parted as he bent to kiss

her, but Leigh raised two hands and pushed hard at his chest, breaking his grip.'

'I want to go home.' She gulped and continued hurriedly, 'This evening was a mistake. I was carried away, and I'm sorry. I promise it won't happen again. I'm not interested in having an affair with you. This was a moment's madness, it didn't mean anything.'

'What the hell are you talking about?' he demanded roughly, the cold anger in his face making her back away. 'Are you playing some kind of game? What makes you think I'm interested in having an affair? It's true I'm not one of your lily-livered boys grateful for a chaste kiss, but equally I'm not a bloody gigolo making love to any female who passes by.' He stopped and rubbed his brow. 'I don't understand, why this sudden about-turn? You're a very desirable woman, and a passionate one. You wanted me as much as I wanted you. You can't change your mind now and pretend it didn't happen, that it meant nothing. What in hell's name am I supposed to do, take a cold shower?' Roughly he reached out and caught her jaw in his strong fingers, holding her close, forcing her to look up into his angry face.

'Yes.' Her voice was low. The vehemence of his reaction had unnerved her. The excuses, the explanation for her behaviour which had seemed so reasonable just a minute ago, now sounded false and trite. Leigh struggled to release herself from his grasp, but it was impossible. His fingers bit into her jaw, creating angry red weals on her skin.

'What are you, some kind of tease?' he sneered.

'It was an animal reaction. I couldn't help myself,' she replied in quivering tones.

'Animal reaction!' his voice shook with fury. 'Is that what I am to you, a bloody animal?' He released her so suddenly that she almost fell. His face was black with rage. He rubbed a hand savagely across the back of his neck, trying to control himself, and she thought for a moment he was going to strike her. She shrank back.

'How was I supposed to react when you responded so

readily in my arms?' he demanded. 'Shake your hand and send you away with a kiss on the cheek. You're not a virgin and you're certainly not frigid. We've both been married before, we're not amateurs. The time is past for playing the shy ingénue. Why didn't you make it clear at the start that you didn't want to make love? I wouldn't have forced you—I would have respected your feelings.' His eyes were like ice chips. 'Perhaps you imagined it would be fun to see how ardent I would become before you slapped me down?' he snarled. 'I've always wanted to make love to you. I envied Patrick—it was blatantly obvious you made him very happy. He couldn't wait to rush home and get into bed with you.'

Leigh stiffened at his words. 'Yes,' she admitted triumphantly, 'it was good between Patrick and me.' She saw the pain in his eyes. 'Very good. But I haven't allowed anyone to touch me since he died. The wine and brandy this evening lowered my resistance, and I would have fallen into the arms of any man.'

'You dare to tell me it wouldn't have mattered a damn who it was, so long as it was male?' Jake gave a bark of grim laughter. 'What a fool I've been! I thought we had something going for us, but now I see how wrong I was. You just used that delicious body of yours to entice me, to satisfy some twisted need, but I was unimportant. Well, you're nothing better than a whore!'

She shrank back from the vile accusation. 'No,' she pleaded.

He glared at her, his chest rising and falling in his fury. The silence was deafening. His eyes roamed her face and body as though he was reliving the naked feel and taste of her. 'I could kill you,' he ground out. Leigh trembled, nailed to the spot by his piercing eyes. There was the sound of a car outside in the drive, the headlights flashed across the windows.

'Who the hell's that?' Jake growled. Quickly he turned on his heel and strode across to fling open the front door as though thankful to have cause to desert her. The engine was cut, then suddenly he gave a bellow and disappeared out into the darkness. Leigh didn't know what to do. Slowly she walked towards the door, and waited hesitantly in the shadows of the porch. Jake was bending over a sleek sports car, and even from a distance the fury of his powerful body was plain to see as he loomed above the driver. 'What, in heaven's name, are you doing here?' he demanded in a low, altogether dangerous tone. The man in the driving seat shifted in the shadows and to her astonishment Leigh realised it was Rory. There was another dark figure beside him.

'The planes for Taiwan were full, and I couldn't book a seat.' The reply was tossed back smoothly.

'Don't be bloody ridiculous!' Jake sliced out the words like knives, greasing each one with scorn. He jerked his head towards the passenger in the front seat. 'I've warned you before—*keep away from her*. I damn well mean it. If I catch you with her again, so help me, I'll give you a thrashing you won't forget!'

'We met on the road. I was giving her a lift.'

'*Liar!*'

Rory shrugged.

Jake looked across at the girl in the car. 'Go inside,' he said, his voice suddenly gentle. The girl rose awkwardly, and Leigh saw she was carrying a baby. As she walked into the pool of light by the front door her distress was apparent. Tears were running down her cheeks, and her nose was pink, but even so she was beautiful. This must be Choo. It was easy to understand Jake's jealousy. She was a small slim Chinese girl in a figure-hugging red brocade cheongsam. Her straight polished black hair hung almost to her waist and her face was dominated by two huge dark almond-shaped eyes. She hitched the baby up further in her arms and gave a sob, walking straight into the hall without a glance at Leigh.

'Don't you ever come to my house again,' Jake threatened menacingly, leaning towards Rory, 'or you'll leave on a stretcher!'

'Your house?' The younger man gave a sneer of empty laughter. 'But it's not *your* house, Jake, is it? It happens to belong to *my* father's company, and you can rest assured that the very minute I become Chairman is the very minute you get kicked out.'

Rory switched on the ignition, the engine roared, and the car shot away.

For a long moment Jake stood in the dark driveway, the muscles of his back moving restlessly, then he turned. 'Come on,' he growled at Leigh, 'I'll take you home.'

CHAPTER FIVE

WITH trembling legs Leigh climbed into the car and sat stiffly erect, her hands gripped tightly in her lap. Deliberately she kept close to the door, away from Jake, determined not to allow the slightest brush of his shoulder or rub of his thigh against hers. She wanted no more bodily contact. He shot her one fierce look as though he wished her a thousand miles away, then manhandled the wheel and swung the Mercedes out on to the lane without a word. She didn't know if he was still mad at her, or at Rory, or both, but what did it matter? A sideways glance revealed that his face was sinister, a pulse throbbing in the clenched set of his jaw. He ignored her completely, and within minutes they were back into the thick of the traffic.

Leigh's head seethed with the evening's surprises. Jake obviously applied a double standard when it came to his behaviour and that of Choo. He felt himself free to see other women, and yet was bitterly possessive, disallowing her the same freedom. The venom in his voice when he had threatened Rory had been real enough. What a typical male chauvinist he was, she decided scornfully. Choo was to remain his sole property, while he made love to other women whenever and wherever he chose. She squirmed as she realised how embarrassing it would have been if the Chinese girl had walked into the house earlier. Suppose she had discovered them together on the sofa! Leigh flushed at the thought and turned angrily to him, her grey eyes darkened to slate. 'Why did you make love to me when Choo was likely to return at any time? Did you want her to find us together, or don't you give a damn about her feelings—or mine?'

'I don't know what you mean,' he rejoined curtly, focusing on the road ahead. 'She wasn't due back until

91

around midnight. The only reason she arrived home earlier was because she had that so-called lift. Besides, I had no idea you and I would fall into each other's arms—it just happened. It certainly wasn't premeditated. Do you imagine I asked you to dinner with the sole intent of seducing you?' He was grimly mocking. 'I can assure you if lovemaking is all I require I can find it in a good many other places, with women who are a darn sight more straightforward than you.' His tone was insolent. Leigh averted her head and stared out into the night, distractedly turning her wedding ring round and round on her finger. She had been right to hate him. Right now she wanted to hit him, throw something at that darkly glowering face. Why should he consider *he* had the right to be so angry? He had trampled over her feelings, and Choo's, without mercy. He was utterly selfish, Leigh smouldered, taking whatever he wanted and to hell with everyone else.

She ignored him for the remainder of the journey and when they arrived at the apartment slammed from the car without a backward glance. It was a relief to discover Frank and Bridget had retired to bed, releasing her from the effort of making polite conversation. It was doubtful she would have made sense anyhow, her nerves were in shreds. She was grateful for the undemanding privacy of her bedroom, and hastily threw off her clothes and lay down, silently fuming. How stupid she had been, allowing Jake's kisses and wandering hands to mislead her. Soberly she recognised that part of the blame was hers; her body had betrayed her. Thank goodness Benjy had woken when he did—it had been a blessing in disguise. Leigh shuddered at the prospect of what would have happened if there had been no interruption. She knew she would have given herself to Jake completely. It had been a lucky escape. There was now only one sensible thing to do—she must keep well away from him.

Leigh gathered from Frank's conversation that Jake had left early the next morning for Penang and was relieved to know he was out of the country. Singapore was only a small island, and the prospect of un-expectedly bumping into him filled her with alarm. Rory too was absent, having obtained a spare seat on a morning flight to Taiwan. In the interim Bridget had suggested a blind date with some friend of a friend of a friend, but Leigh briskly put her foot down. There had been enough problems with the opposite sex already during her holiday; all she wanted to do now was bask in the sunshine and lead an uncomplicated life.

Rory came back at the weekend and whisked her off to dinner and dancing. He made no mention of the confrontation at Jake's, and Leigh wondered if he realised she had been there. Presumably Jake had also returned to be with Benjy, but his name was never mentioned. She was annoyed with herself for even bothering to wonder about him and made a determined effort to concentrate on less provocative topics, but it was difficult. Jake had a nasty habit of creeping into her thoughts when she was least expecting it.

She was climbing out of the pool a couple of days later after a refreshing dip when Bridget appeared and settled herself at the poolside table beneath the shade of a red and white striped umbrella. She watched as Leigh picked up a towel and stretched out on the grass in her bikini.

'You know you've always wanted to go to Hong Kong,' Bridget bubbled, 'well, now's your chance!'

Leigh regarded her with suspicion, her grey eyes clouded. What scheme was her hostess hatching up now?

'Jake has been on the phone. He has to visit Hong Kong unexpectedly to get the contract agreed. As director of the company he must put his signature on the document when the order is finalised. Apparently things have moved faster than anticipated. Rory's cock-a-hoop at the chance to have it all signed, sealed and delivered before Sir Clive flies here next week.'

'Where do I come in?' Leigh asked, puzzled.

'Apparently there's one more meeting before the thing is finally settled, to clarify a few points, and Jake needs someone along to take notes. He asked if you would be prepared to go.'

'*Me?*' She felt prickles of alarm move along her spine. 'Why not Sunantha?'

'She's off work. Her mother's ill.'

'Can't he use a tape recorder or something?' she asked, trying to mask her agitation.

'No, he needs someone there to act as a witness, someone who does shorthand. He doesn't trust Jimmy Tay. He thinks he might still try and pull a fast one, even at this late stage.'

'But surely Rory has everything arranged?'

'Almost, but not quite. Anyhow, Jake asked specifically if you would do him, Rory and the company a great favour by going along.'

Leigh sat up and hugged her bare legs. 'I don't know,' she said, her eyes troubled. It seemed remarkable that Jake would want anything more to do with her after their last heated fracas. Then she realised with a sudden surge of anger that *he* didn't need her at all, the company did. He was obviously prepared to ignore his feelings, and hers, for the sake of a hefty chunk of profit. A leopard never changes its spots, she thought bitterly.

'If you don't go he'll have to postpone the visit until Sunantha returns, and that means Sir Clive will have been and gone. Rory will be so disappointed if he can't produce the signed contract to show his father.'

Leigh rubbed the towel slowly over her wet arms. 'How long would it be for?' she asked thoughtfully.

'Only two or three days.'

Her head spun with uncertainties. What was the point in meeting up with Jake again when they couldn't even be together for five minutes before one or other of them lost their temper?

'Jake'll probably be tied up most of the time,' Bridget told her, 'but you'll be able to do some sightseeing on your own. He'll arrange a guide. Please say you'll go.'

'Well, I don't know . . .'

'Thanks, I knew you'd agree.' Bridget was up and out of her chair in a flash. 'I'll give Jake a ring and let him know. He'll arrange the tickets and accommodation.' She gave a chuckle. 'I know you'll both enjoy yourselves!'

In double quick time it was all fixed for Leigh to meet Jake at Changi Airport the following morning for their flight out to Hong Kong, and when Rory took her out dancing that evening he was brimming with delight. 'Thanks for your help. This order means a great deal to me, and the sooner it's finalised the better.' He reached into his jacket and pulled out a flat, rectangular packet. 'Would you do me another favour? Would you give this to Jimmy Tay?'

She looked at him questioningly.

'It's a crocodile skin wallet. Jimmy's treated me to some wonderful nights out, wining and dining, in the past, and I want to say thank you.' He handed her the packet. 'The wallet is special—it's Italian styled, highly exclusive and very expensive. Look after it carefully, and don't bother to tell Jake. He'd be furious. He doesn't like Jimmy, and if he realised just how friendly we are he'd blow his top. He doesn't approve of mixing business with pleasure.'

Leigh tucked the packet away in her handbag. Jake's jealousy over Choo appeared to have soured his whole relationship with Rory. 'Don't worry,' she smiled, 'I'll slip it to Mr Tay when Jake isn't looking.'

'Good girl!'

When Yacob delivered her to the airport before eight the next morning Jake was already waiting, tall and forceful in a beautifully cut dark brown suit and beige shirt. He greeted her coolly, wearing the face of a polite stranger which gave no indication of his feelings. A pretty girl from the travel agents graciously tended to their baggage and tickets, and whisked them aboard the jet ahead of other waiting passengers with a minimum of fuss. Jake calmly accepted this special treatment without comment. He was used to being cossetted, and he settled down in his seat in the first class cabin with just a murmur of thanks before becoming quickly engrossed in the financial section of the morning paper.

Leigh, on the other hand, had never travelled in such luxury. She looked around, noting the air of affluence, the wide comfortable seats, the space, the elegant hostesses standing by to satisfy every possible whim of the passengers.

'I always go first class,' Jake commented with a flicker of amusement as she drank it all in with wide blue eyes. 'I travel so much I reckon I deserve to do it in comfort. I get through a hell of a lot of paperwork on planes.'

A smiling steward appeared with a tray of glasses, and Leigh looked across at him in surprise. Surely it was too early in the day for anything alcoholic?

'Would madam care for a drink?' He bowed solicitously.

'Yes, madam would,' Jake said firmly, and handed her a glass of champagne, his eyes daring her to resist. He took whisky for himself.

'It was very decent of you to suggest that you join me,' he commented, watching with a wry smile as she wrinkled her nose at the bubbles. 'It's pulled us out of one hell of a spot.'

She looked across at him in astonishment over the top of the glass. '*I* didn't suggest anything,' she retorted coldly.

He gave her a quizzical glance. 'But Bridget told me it was all your idea, you wanted to help.'

Leigh set her lips into a thin line. 'It was *you* who asked me to come, not the other way round. Bridget had to plead with me to agree. You don't imagine I would have come of my own accord, do you?'

The corner of his mouth twitched. 'That's not very flattering, I thought you couldn't resist me.'

'Well, I can,' she said waspishly.

'What a shame, and here I was with high hopes!' He was laughing at her. Leigh blushed at the suggestiveness of his words.

'It's obvious there's been some kind of mistake.' She looked round wildly.

He put his hand on her knee. 'You can't change your mind now, we're about to take off.'

As the plane began its race along the runway Leigh removed his hand and took another frantic gulp of champagne. 'I thought you needed a witness and someone to take notes.'

'I do,' he told her in a calm assured voice, 'but I could have asked one of the other secretaries. It was only because Bridget said you were desperate to see Hong Kong and begged me to take you along that I agreed.' He leaned towards her. 'You *do* want to see Hong Kong, don't you?'

'Yes,' she said weakly. The plane thrust itself up into the sky.

Jake gave a low chuckle. 'You've got to hand it to old Bridget, she's worked a flanker this time. I wouldn't be surprised if she's telephoned ahead, cancelled our separate bedrooms and ordered the bridal suite!'

Leigh's head swam. The plane banked steeply and the pull of gravity forced her back in her seat. Jake's amusement was disconcerting. He had accepted the situation too readily. He was usually furious about Bridget's interference, but this time he didn't appear to resent it at all, indeed he seemed to have awarded her top marks for trying.

'Aren't you angry?' she asked.

He moved a shoulder in an eloquent gesture. 'Why should I be? I'm going to Hong Kong to sign a million-dollar contract with a beautiful young woman by my side, what more could I want?' The plane levelled out. He reached across and ran one finger down her cheek in a slow, sensuous path. 'This is third time lucky.' She looked at him with puzzled eyes. 'The first two occasions that we've been together have been fraught with disaster, to say the least.' He cocked an ironical brow. 'I sincerely hope this time we can make a go of it.'

Leigh was instantly wary. That mocking smile was flickering at the corner of his mouth again. She mistrusted his affability, it would have been altogether preferable if he had been coolly indifferent.

'I don't know what you mean,' she retorted in schoolmarmish tones.

He laughed and with long fingers gently turned her face to his. 'You know very well,' he insisted quietly, and leant forward to brush her lips with his in a tender caress that sent her senses reeling and made it perfectly clear what he had in mind. 'It will be better in Hong Kong,' he said with confident smugness. 'We'll be alone, no little boys to disturb us, no unexpected visitors.'

'I—I don't want to,' she stammered. His words, his gaze, the fingers which stroked her skin, were pulling her inexorably down into a quicksand of heady desire.

'Don't you?' His eyes were penetrating her very soul, stripping away her lies, her inhibitions, reducing her to unquestioning obedience. 'You wanted to the other night. If we hadn't been disturbed you would have gone to bed with me,' he drawled silkily, and the certainty in his blue eyes quelled any denial. 'It was only because we were interrupted that you changed your mind. I'm sorry I lost my temper, but you have to admit I had cause. This time, however, I shall make certain there are no intrusions.'

Leigh swallowed hard, trying to find the strength for retaliation, but it was beyond her. His arrogant assurance that she was willing to surrender to him took her breath away. Surely she hadn't been completely abandoned in his arms the other evening? Her mind raced back in confusion. He had totally the wrong idea.

'I don't want to get involved,' she heard herself say in a thin, uncertain voice.

Jake put his hand over hers and was just about to whisper something in her ear, something which she knew had to be intimate, full of his supreme male self-confidence, when a large, florid-faced man in his forties loomed above them in the aisle.

'Hello, Jake, my old friend!' He proffered a fat hand with thick fingers.

'Good morning, Carl,' Jake replied pleasantly, though Leigh noticed his smile didn't reach his eyes. 'This is Mr de Groot, a business colleague,' he explained briefly. The man nodded at Leigh and turned again to Jake.

'I believe we are both on the same errand?' His words

were heavily accented. 'Both doing our best, by fair means or foul, to secure a profitable order.'

Jake made a noncommittal movement of his head. It was obvious he was not prepared to indulge in a spontaneous business discussion.

'Jimmy Tay is a plausible character, isn't he?' the man continued, his beady eyes searching Jake's expression for some clue as to his feelings. 'I would rather do business with a rattlesnake.' His voice dropped. 'The only way to make sure of the business is to line his pocket, I think.'

Jake looked up at him steadily, his eyes a steely gray. 'Low prices and good delivery dates play a part,' he commented drily.

'Don't the British stoop to bribery and corruption, then?' Mr de Groot gave a loud bellow of laughter which made several other passengers turn their heads to look at him.

'I don't.' The reply was snapped out.

The man shifted uncomfortably. There was a long pause. 'Well, it has been nice talking to you,' he muttered as it became obvious Jake was not about to contribute anything further. He bowed at Leigh. 'And to your beautiful wife.'

She was about to open her mouth to explain his mistake when there was the warning bite of Jake's hard fingers on her wrist. She hesitated. Mr de Groot smiled a plastic farewell and returned to his seat three rows ahead.

'Why didn't you tell him I was your secretary?' she hissed as the Dutchman sat down.

'Do you think he'd believe that?' Jake gave a soft snort of derision. 'He knows Sunantha, and he's aware that European secretaries aren't allowed work permits in Singapore. He'd just think we were off for a few days of lust and debauchery.'

Leigh was tempted to reply that Jake seemed to think that, too, but she held her tongue.

'He'd love to be able to snigger about me behind my back,' he continued, 'but I have a respectable reputation

in the business world. Bridget might trot out the odd
innuendo, but the facts speak for themselves. There's
never been a breath of scandal about me or the company, and there never will be. I also care about Benjy
and his moral standards. I would never do anything to
cause scurrilous gossip.'

'What about us?' she accused hotly.

The smile twitched at the corner of his mouth again.
'*That*, my beautiful girl, is very different. I can assure
you my intentions are completely honourable.'

'I don't believe you!'

'That's up to you.' He reached into his inside jacket
pocket and pulled out a pack of cigars. 'Do you mind if
I smoke?'

Leigh shook her head, chewing over his words. Jake
lit the cigar and took a deep inward breath. 'It's odd,'
he mused, exhaling slowly, 'from what de Groot says it
sounds as though the contract isn't as tied up as Rory
indicated. I wonder if Jimmy's been angling for some
kind of pay-off? Hell, I hope Rory's handled him
properly.' He ran his fingers through his thick hair in
agitation. 'I deliberately left him alone on this deal, I
wonder if I did the right thing.' He rotated the cigar
slowly in his fingers. 'However, I won't bore you with
business,' his glance was flecked with wry laughter, 'I
know you wouldn't be impressed. How about some
coffee?'

The remainder of the journey passed pleasantly
enough. As promised Jake made no further reference to
business, or to what he expected of their time together.
Instead he kept the conversation on a pleasant, easy
level, talking of the different countries he had visited,
and asking about her work in England. 'Almost there.'
He studied the heavy watch on his wrist. They were
approaching Hong Kong's Kai Tak airport. Leigh
looked out of the window and gasped. The plane was so
low that they seemed to be flying alongside the housing
blocks and skyscrapers which grew up from the mainland like stalagmites. The buildings were only a wingtip
away.

Jake smiled at her surprise. 'Incredible, isn't it? And here's Fragrant Harbour.' Leigh looked at him questioningly. 'That's what Hong Kong means in English,' he explained.

The plane dropped lower and lower, then she saw the sea. For a moment it appeared as though they were destined to land on water, but at the last moment the wheels hit the grey tarmac of the runway and they slowly ran down to a halt.

'There'll be a mile-long queue at Customs,' Jake said, ruefully, as he took her elbow and steered her through baggage collection. 'Don't get upset if they fling out your undies for everyone to see. They take a delight in inspecting everything in fine detail.'

After a ten-minute wait they reached the Customs bench. Leigh went ahead of him. She set down her case and reached to unlock it. The Customs official flicked his eyes appreciatively over her slender body in the cream linen suit. 'First time in Hong Kong?' he asked, with such a bright smile that she decided the Chinese weren't inscrutable after all.

Leigh grinned back. 'It is, and I know I'm going to enjoy it.'

'Hope you do,' he said, 'wish I could show you around. Anything to declare?'

'No.'

He gave her a cheery wink and jerked his head. 'Off you go, you look honest.'

He held out a restraining hand for Jake's luggage. Leigh walked forward a few yards and then paused by the barrier to wait, laughing as Jake shrugged his shoulders at her in a gesture of mock defeat when the Customs man opened the lid of his suitcase. His belongings were examined thoroughly, but he acquiesced with patient resignation, and then, when the official was satisfied, thrust several overhanging items roughly back into his case and snapped down the locks. 'How come you get by scot-free?' he asked as he joined her, his eyes gleaming. 'That's inequality of the sexes for you! Just because you're female and very sexy.'

'I thought I was foxy?' she teased, her head on one side, her tongue protruding a little way between her white teeth.

His eyes roved her body, undressing her shamefully until she lost her nerve and walked forward.

'Benjy told you that, didn't he?' he queried, moving alongside her with easy strides. 'I was talking about you, and happened to say you were a foxy lady.'

'And that took more explaining than the word "atmosphere"?'

'It sure did.'

He guided her through the busy corridors to the pick-up area. 'How about some sightseeing this afternoon?'

'With you?' Leigh couldn't keep the surprise from her voice. She'd understood he would be working.

'Who else do you have in mind?' he grinned. 'And then this evening we'll have dinner and I'll brief you on tomorrow's meeting. It's fixed for ten in the morning, and if all goes well Jimmy Tay and I should sign on the dotted line after lunch.' He frowned. 'If all goes well.'

A silver Rolls-Royce purred forward. Leigh's eyes were as round as saucers.

'Don't look so impressed,' Jake laughed as he gave her a gentle push. She climbed into its elegant luxury feeling like Cinderella stepping into her silver coach. 'It's from the hotel,' he explained. 'They send it for other guests too, not just me. It's a gimmick.'

Leigh stroked the smooth grey leather panelling with respect. 'An expensive gimmick. It beats plastic toys in cornflakes!'

The Rolls took them through the Cross Harbour Tunnel which links Kowloon with Hong Kong Island. Their hotel was on the inward side of the island, looking across Victoria Harbour to the mainland. After registering they had a quick lunch and went up to their rooms to change. Leigh pulled on classic blue jeans and a bright red tee-shirt. She bundled her hair up on to the top of her head, and after a hasty whisk of the mascara brush she was ready. There was so much to see and do. When Jake knocked she was engrossed in the view from the window. 'Isn't it exciting?' she grinned as he joined her. He, too, was casually dressed in faded jeans and a short-sleeved navy shirt. The cool and capable business executive had vanished with his change of clothes, and he seemed younger, easygoing and much more approachable. Together they gazed across at the crowded shores of Kowloon, with its jungle of buildings and crammed streets. The Star Ferry chugged over the narrow strip of water in the distance.

'The mountains belong to China.' Jake pointed to the jagged backdrop of hazy blue peaks. 'If there's time I'll take you to Lok Ma Chau, that's one of the border crossings in the New Territories.'

She turned to him, her grey eyes shining. 'Thank you for bringing me.'

'Thank Bridget,' he said cryptically. 'Come on—I've rustled up a hire car, we're going to Aberdeen.'

Aberdeen was unique. It was a fishing village on the southern shore of Hong Kong Island, overlooking the wide blue stretch of the South China Sea which glimmered like diamonds in the hot sun. Leigh had never seen anything like it before. The village heaved with noisy, smelly, vibrating life. The harbour was thronged with boats, all anchored side by side, forming a vast swaying community connected by narrow gangplanks. There were large boats and small boats, new ones, and many which seemed to be nailed together with a smile and a prayer. And the boats were homes; they were alive with people. Yellow-skinned babies tottered on the decks, wizened Chinese grannies sat solemnly alongside chicken coops, washing hung from poles, children danced around jumbles of rope, eyes peered from gloomy cabins. Leigh gripped Jake's arm in her excitement.

'Glad you came?' he asked, kissing her forehead.

'Oh yes!' she breathed, hardly noticing his caress as her big eyes darted backwards and forwards. He laughed and put his arm around her shoulders, hugging her tight.

'That's my beautiful girl,' he said, enjoying her

delight. His words sent a sudden flicker of alarm through her slender frame. She was allowing her pleasure to distract her. Carefully she disengaged herself from him, and he dropped his arm. 'Why are you always on guard?' he asked perspicaciously. 'You have nothing to fear from me.'

'I'm not on guard,' she assured him shakily, and walked quickly ahead so that he couldn't read the doubt in her eyes.

After Aberdeen Jake took them to Repulse Bay where they had afternoon tea in an elegant white stuccoed hotel overlooking the water. Then, as the sun was setting, he drove them to the Peak and they parked the car and strolled along the path to the very crest of the hill. It was like being on top of the world. The views were spectacular—the wide greeny-blue sea, the pinks and golds of the setting sun, the unrelenting harshness of the mountains of Kwangtung Province, the acres of straining concrete below them hurtling down the hillside towards the sea. Neon lights of hotels and bars began to flicker brightly in the dusk. As night fell over the scatter of islands and the mighty mainland they stood and watched. Again Jake put his arm around her, but this time Leigh relaxed and leant against him, then, almost without realising it, she clasped his waist and smiled up at him. When darkness came they were alone in the balmy evening. His lips moved slowly over her forehead, and he bent his tawny head and kissed her mouth. Her lips parted beneath his, and the taste of him awakened a need. She curled her fingers around his neck and sighed. The excitement of Hong Kong merged into the excitement of him—his mouth exploring hers, his fingers moving urgently across her back. 'I wish you'd wear a bra under that damn tee-shirt,' he muttered. 'The thought of your naked breasts is driving me insane!' He touched the thin cotton, then abruptly wrenched himself away. 'Not here,' he said, taking her hand. 'Let's go and have some dinner.'

He started to run, pulling her with him, until she gave a laughing shout of protest at his speed.

Leigh hadn't realised how hungry she was until she was handed the menu. It resembled a small book with its dark maroon velvet cover and parchment pages. After a great deal of deliberation she decided upon Sole Véronique with wild rice and courgettes. Jake settled for pepper steak, medium rare. He had selected a bottle of white wine from the list, which they both enjoyed. The waiter removed their empty plates and produced a second, smaller menu.

'No dessert for me,' Leigh said with a smile, 'I'm full.'

Jake indicated that he, too, would forgo another course and ordered coffee and liqueurs. Leigh leant back in her chair and surveyed the hotel restaurant. It was elegantly plush, with dark panelled walls, red velvet chairs and crystal wall-lights. A piano tinkled discreetly in the background. 'I think I could easily adapt to a life of luxury,' she smiled.

'And I think I could easily adapt to *you*,' he murmured, reaching across and touching her fingers. Her heart skidded as he traced a slow, sensuous pattern in her palm. His eyes slid down from her face to her low cleavage and rested there a moment. The afternoon's sun had deepened the golden glow of her tan, and in the soft light she looked almost sultry. She was wearing a white satin halter-neck dress with a deep vee. The skirt was tight, with a split almost to mid-thigh, and a slender gold kid belt encircled her waist. She wore a pair of matching golden bangles around one upper arm.

'Tell me about tomorrow's meeting.' Leigh moved her fingers from Jake's in a determined effort to resist the electricity which was flowing between them. Again, as when she had dined with him before, she sensed an undercurrent of emotion whipping them tightly together, and it unsettled her. 'What exactly do you want me to do?' she asked, trying to divert their relationship on to a more businesslike footing.

Jake regarded her for a long moment, then lit a cigar. 'I want you to try and merge into the background, if that's at all possible.' He glanced again at the tantalising curves and grinned. 'For heaven's sake wear something that isn't too revealing, otherwise I shall have trouble concentrating! Keep a low profile and perhaps Jimmy Tay will forget you're taking notes. I want everything recorded, especially what *he* says.' Jake narrowed his eyes and frowned. 'The more I think about de Groot's comments, the more convinced I am that something is wrong. Rory was certain he and Jimmy had everything finalised between them, but I'm beginning to wonder. I have the contract all typed out ready to be signed, but I'm not putting my name to anything until I'm completely satisfied all the details are in order.'

Leigh said nothing. She remembered Rory's gift lying in her suitcase. It could prove difficult to pass over during the morning's meeting, but perhaps there would be an opportunity in the afternoon, when Jake was busy signing the contract. She wondered why he disliked Rory so much. His voice inevitably took on a hard cutting edge when he mentioned him. Probably it's because Rory is the Chairman's son, she thought scornfully. Jake is jealous. It seemed an ungracious emotion for such a powerful character, but he was only human after all.

A misty spiral rose from Jake's cigar and floated in the air. 'I don't trust Jimmy one inch,' he continued. 'He'd alter the truth if it suited him. I'll feel much happier if the entire exchange is put down in black and white, just as a safeguard in case there's any dispute in the future. At least he's not likely to push for anything underhand while you're there, thank goodness, though who knows what he's suggested to Rory.' He tapped away the ash, and set his jaw into an angular tightness. 'If Rory's not told me the truth about this deal I'll murder the bastard!' The savage look on his tanned face indicated his fury.

'Why don't you like him?'

Jake glanced across at her through thick dark lashes. 'I don't care for nepotism for a start, particularly as Rory isn't cut out to be a businessman. He'll allow the company to slide. It breaks my heart to think of the years of effort which will go down the drain just because he's too busy playing rugby or whatever to devote some time to Milwain International.' He gave an impatient snort. 'The company provides a living, in one way or another, for thousands of people throughout the world—employees and shareholders, and at the end of the day they depend upon a competent Chairman.'

'And you don't think Rory will be competent?'

'I bloody *know* he won't,' he flashed. The hard line to his jaw only began to soften when Leigh steered the conversation on to other topics. Jake signalled the waiter and charged the bill to his account.

'Would you like to go dancing?' he asked, as she walked ahead of him from the restaurant.

'I didn't think you'd waste time on such frivolity, Jake!' Leigh cast an impertinent glance over her shoulder. 'Don't you want to check over your papers for tomorrow?'

He reached forward and grabbed her arm with a large hand, swinging her round to face him. 'That just proves how little you know about me. I don't work twenty-four hours a day,' he retaliated. 'I do allow myself some pleasures.' His eyes travelled down her body in an outright statement of the pleasures he desired. Leigh could feel the static in the air.

'I'm tired,' she decided quickly, desperate to escape the gleam in his eye, the powerful aura of his vibrant masculinity. 'I think I'll turn in for the night.'

'Okay.' There was a sardonic lift to his brow. 'Whatever you wish.'

They travelled up together in the lift and as Leigh reached her room she hurriedly took out her key from the white satin clutch bag and unlocked the door. 'Goodnight, thank you for a nice evening,' she gabbled. Even to herself she sounded like a shy schoolgirl returning from her first date, so great was her wish to get away from him, to be safe.

Jake laughed under his breath, amused by her sudden confusion. 'Aren't you going to offer me a drink?'

'A drink?' She looked blank.

'There's a fridge in your room,' he explained patiently,

as though speaking to a small, not particularly bright
child, 'which contains a selection of booze. We'll have a
nightcap. I'll have gin and tonic, and while you're pouring it I'll go next door to my room and bring you some
advertising guff.'

'What for?' Leigh knew she sounded stupid, but for
the life of her she couldn't compose her thoughts quickly
enough to grasp what he was talking about. His proximity, his calm, cool authority was pushing her into a
maze of indecision, where she was only certain of one
thing. She didn't want to give him a drink because she
didn't want him *in her bedroom*.

'To help you grasp some of the technical terms used in
the earth-moving business,' he said reasonably, 'then it
will be easier when you are taking it all down in shorthand tomorrow.'

'Oh.'

He grinned down at her bemused expression and left.

Leigh snapped on all the switches she could find, but
still the room remained alarmingly dim and seductive.
There was no central light, only one ceramic standard
lamp and a matching one on the chest of drawers. There
was a thin strip of neon above the mirror, but she turned
that off hastily. She had no wish to see her reflection
side by side with Jake's. The soft light made her wonder
if the hotel had designed the rooms especially for cland-
estine meetings. Leigh took a deep breath. She was
overreacting again.

The fridge was easily located neatly concealed within
an elegant fitment of drawers and cupboards. With
shaking hands she poured his gin. She mustn't let him
touch her, even the caress of his fingers on hers sent fire
leaping in her blood. Leigh knew she would be unable
to resist him. For two barren years she had managed to
live without sexual love, but now she was vulnerable—
oh so very vulnerable! She poured out a stiff brandy
and took a large mouthful, making herself splutter. She
wiped her lips with the back of her hand. This feeling of
danger was ridiculous. There was no need at all to fear
Jake's presence. She only had to say no. It wasn't as

though she even *liked* him particularly. After all, how could you like a man who had been directly involved in your husband's death? Be truthful, Leigh Nicholas, she told herself sternly. You'd never be in this state if you didn't like him. You like him a lot, in fact far more than any other man you've met during the past two years, and from the way you're behaving you're showing all the signs of becoming just as infatuated with him as Sunantha.

And as far as blaming him for Patrick's death is concerned, well, surely it's about time that old grievance was dumped where it belongs—in the deep blue sea. Patrick's death was an accident. Patrick would never have wanted her to blame Jake. In fact he would probably be delighted if she and Jake continued the friendship which had existed between them. She gave a sigh and walked across to the window to pull aside the long curtains, gazing out at the night. The gaudy reds and blues of neon signs on the mainland were reflected in the deep black waters of the harbour. She took another swift gulp of brandy.

'Here they are,' Jake tossed some glossy leaflets on to the chest of drawers. He had removed his jacket to reveal a short-sleeved shirt in pale grey poplin. The fine golden hairs on his forearms glinted in the light as he picked up his glass. 'Thanks,' he said, taking a mouthful. He joined her at the window, putting his hand casually on her shoulder, and she trembled, the glass shaking in her grasp. 'For heaven's sake,' he grinned, 'I'm not about to rape you! Give me that.' He took the glass from her and set it down firmly alongside the leaflets. Then he put both hands on her shoulders and pulled her back into the room, away from the window. 'Kiss me.'

'No . . . . I . . . . Oh no,' she stumbled through the protestations, shaking her head in confusion. The burning look in his heavy-lidded eyes was reducing her to a quivering wreck. He pulled her closer.

'Drop your guard, Leigh, you can't hide behind it for ever. Don't deny what you feel. Take chances. Be honest.'

'Are you?' she challenged weakly.

'Perhaps I'm not always completely honest unless it suits me,' Jake admitted, his fingers feverishly caressing her smooth tanned shoulders. 'Dishonesty by omission, I suppose you could call it.' He moved his gaze from hers, frowning a little.

'Well then?' she countered.

His eyes swept back to her and he gave an uncharacteristically tentative smile. 'I didn't mean to say this so soon, but I suppose I'd better be honest about how I feel.' He hesitated, then swallowed hard. 'I love you, my beautiful girl. I've loved you for a long time.' He touched her forehead with burning lips and his fingers gripped her shoulders. 'Leigh, I want you so much! Whenever I touch you I drive myself crazy. I can't stop thinking about you.' He gave a dry laugh. 'I thought I was too old to feel like this again, but I do.' He kissed her cheek. 'And not, my darling, it's your turn to be honest, take chances.'

Leigh looked down. Jake's talk of love was confusing. She felt as though she was on a roller-coaster, being carried along breathlessly at great speed, not knowing whether she should laugh or cry.

'Drop your guard,' he insisted quietly. 'We're on our own, just you and me in the whole world. Forget the past, forget everything, it's you and me together, here, now.'

Leigh moved restlessly. Her whole body cried out for him.

'Kiss me,' he demanded huskily, '*you* kiss *me*.'

As though in a dream she raised her lips to Jake's, tasting his sweetness, then his mouth was plundering hers until bugles of desire blared in her head like a crazy chorus. His hands worked across her naked back, and his breathing quickened. He kissed her throat, her shoulders, the swell of her breasts until her skin flamed with the urgency of his touch. 'Jake,' she muttered brokenly, and thrust her arms around his neck, arching her hungry body against him. His mouth returned to hers, hot and fiery and demanding, and then his long fingers were tugging at the knot at the nape of her neck, and the fine fabric of her dress fell away to reveal full tiptilted breasts. His hands covered them possessively and he made a husky sound in the back of his throat. He pushed her gently towards the bed and switched off the light. In the darkness the thump of her heart sounded like a primitive drumbeat. Jake's hands roamed her body, stroking, loving, teasing until she thought she would swoon with desire. Then he trailed his lips downwards until they reached the taut straining nipples. His expert mouth caressed first one and then the other, over and over again. Leigh moaned his name, moving her hands across his wide shoulders, then with shaking fingers she fumbled at the buttons on his shirt.

'Are you sure, Leigh?' He was suddenly calm. His strong hands enclosed hers, preventing any further movement. 'I can stop now—just,' he said throatily in the blackness, 'but if I feel you naked against me I shall have to make love to you, I won't be able to stop then.' He leant across and switched on the bedside lamp. His eyes were hooded, his face gentle. 'If you want to change your mind, my beautiful girl, now's the time to do it. Don't have any doubts.'

She could see the effort it was taking him to control himself, the hard muscles moving restlessly beneath his clothes. 'Be sure, Leigh, be sure.'

All she wanted was Jake, that was all. Jake was the whole world, and the whole world was Jake. She needed to feel him against her, inside her, with her. 'I'm sure,' she groaned.

Jake allowed her to push his hands away and unbutton his shirt, then he stretched out a long arm and snapped off the light. Their clothes were hastily discarded and she sighed, trailing her hands across the broad expanse of his heaving chest. It was wonderful to feel his nakedness. Slowly they explored each other's bodies, whispering words of love, playing a sensual game which provoked in Leigh an ecstasy beyond belief. The urgency built relentlessly. She could feel Jake's leashed strength as he sought to control himself.

'I can't wait any longer, darling,' he gasped, his mouth open against her throat. 'Now, now, *now*!' He was on top of her, his hard muscular body thrusting down fiercely until everything was spinning out of control and the world exploded, tossing her down into a warm dark womb of oblivion where there was nothing but the feel, the scent the touch of Jake inside her skin, inside her soul, part of her. Jake oozing from her pores, drenching her with love.

She slumped beneath him, her mouth slack, a thin film of perspiration on her face. He held her close. 'My love, my love,' he murmured. They lay entwined, exhausted and content until she drifted off into a drowsy, luxurious slumber. Some time later she felt his mouth on her hair, on her shoulders, rousing her gently until she awoke. He took her again, and afterwards Leigh stretched and smiled, she felt so safe, so indolent, so happy. Much later Jake moved from her and looked at his watch. It was the midnight hour.

'I'd better go back to my room, my darling.' His lips stemmed her protest. 'If I stay here all night neither of us will get any sleep,' he said tenderly. 'It's been a long day and I need to have my wits about me in the morning.' Tiredly he pulled on his shirt. 'Also Frank might be trying to reach me. I phoned him earlier this evening, and asked him to check some of the figures on the Tay deal. He was going out, but said he'd try to telephone back either just after midnight or first thing in the morning.' When he was dressed he pulled the covers up to her chin and tucked her in. 'Sleep well, my beautiful girl.' He bent down to her, and Leigh thrust her hands into his hair, pulling him down on top of her.

'Oh Leigh,' he moaned, his mouth moving desperately over her face, his hard body heavy on hers. 'I don't want to go, but I *must*.'

Leigh watched as he reluctantly made his way to the door, and as he smiled goodnight she blew him a kiss.

CHAPTER SIX

LEIGH was dreaming, floating on a soft pink cloud of contentment which made her want to purr. Languorously she stretched and turned over, pulling the blankets around her in a warm cocoon of bliss. She drifted back on to the cloud and smiled.

Abruptly there was noise, making her jump violently in an instinctive reaction against the shrill intrusion that smashed into her consciousness like a brick through a plate glass window. For a moment she was totally disorientated. She shook her head and screwed up her eyes, struggling to wake. Where was she? The noise continued to penetrate as she clawed her way from sleep and realised it was the telephone. She put out a meandering hand and eventually her fingers closed around the receiver and dragged it to her ear.

'Hello?'

'Hello, my beautiful girl. Did you sleep well?'

She muttered something incoherent and Jake laughed.

'Wake up, Leigh! It's eight o'clock. Hurry and get dressed. I'll collect you for breakfast in fifteen minutes. We'll have to get a move on, the meeting's at ten.'

'Okay.' Dropping the receiver haphazardly back on to its cradle, she staggered from the bed and into the bathroom. With a great surge of willpower she switched on the shower, turned the dial to cold and stood beneath it. The impact of the icy water made her gasp. She picked up the soap and began lathering herself briskly. Then, like a thunderbolt, the realisation of what she had done the night before swamped her.

Leigh's elation vanished. Abruptly her hands stopped their work and she gave a tortured groan. How could she have been so abandoned, so wanton, as to allow her wayward emotions to carry her away completely? A

113

queasy feeling of despair infiltrated her being, making her lean against the tiled wall, her heart palpitating like a wild thing. Why on earth had she allowed Jake to make love to her? She must have been out of her mind! For two years she had kept her life on an even keel, but now it had tipped disastrously, and she was in danger of sinking into a sea of emotion, desire and unexpressed needs, when all she really wanted was to sit safely on the shore. And it wasn't as though Jake had had to coax her. He had deliberately offered her the opportunity to stop, which she had refused. Her face grew hot with shame. She rinsed away the soap and began drying herself roughly with a white fluffy towel.

Casual sex had never been on her agenda. She was well aware that her strict moral standards could be interpreted as archaic in this day and age. Many of her girl friends would not consider a holiday complete without a romp with some attractive man, and Jake was certainly that. But she had never viewed sex in that light. To her it was an act of love which only took place between two people who cared for each other, who had built up a cherished relationship. Everything had happened too quickly with Jake, she didn't know whether she was on her head or her heels.

Leigh flung away the towel and started to dress. She and Patrick had gone steady for a year, been engaged six months, and had waited until they were married before putting the final seal on their love. But with Jake, the second man in her life, she had tossed aside convention and followed her heart instead of her head. A sob rose in her throat. She wasn't even sure it was her heart she had followed; there was an uneasy suspicion it had been the needs of her body which had dictated her rash action. She'd been so *easy*! Third time lucky, Jake had said, and that was all it had taken, three meetings before she'd gone to bed with him. She felt like a fallen woman, whatever that meant.

How could she ever face him again? He must be laughing at her, at the weak protests that had turned into passionate cries of desire with a minimum of effort on his part. It was embarrassing. Leigh put on her cream linen suit and fixed her face without scarcely looking at it. Jake must be used to women who showed no compunction in offering themselves to him. She recalled how Bridget had said he had worked his way through females of many different nationalities. The ethnic group he was studying right now must be the British, she thought bitterly; I'm auburn amongst the brunettes. With shaking fingers she pinned back her hair into a smooth pleat and sprayed cologne behind her ears and on the throbbing pulses at her wrists. Automatically the unread advertising leaflets were pushed into a folder, along with pens, pencils and a shorthand notebook. Leigh put her hands to her hot cheeks and swallowed.

Jake had told her he loved her. In all probability he said that to all his women. It was his way of saying, 'I like you enough to sleep with you', but it meant nothing. Their encounter had been merely a brief coming together which they had both enjoyed, but which shouldn't be taken too seriously. Leigh gulped, trying to remove the hard lump of shame that was constricting her throat. She refused to be swept away by love again. It was too soon, and besides, she would only be hurt, especially by a man like Jake, a sophisticated man, a man who used women. It was vital she play things cool, she decided. Act the part of the liberated woman, it was the only way. Her moment of indiscretion must be obliterated as soon as possible, and to do that she must convince Jake it meant nothing to her, then he would leave her alone.

Her head felt hot and heavy with doughballs of emotion. There was a knock at the door, and with a fluttering heart she tucked the folder beneath her arm, picked up her handbag and hastily struggled to adopt a businesslike attitude before opening the door. The dewy-eyed look must be avoided at all costs.

'Good morning,' she said briskly, flashing a cocktail party smile as she marched past him into the corridor. 'Is Jimmy Tay's office far from here?' She strode determinedly down the hallway, acutely conscious of Jake walking at her shoulder, tall and lithe.

'Just a couple of blocks.' He glanced at her quizzically, trying to read her mood. The pert profile was composed.

'I'll do my best to take everything down in shorthand,' she told him in a breezy voice that totally belied the turmoil beneath, 'but I could miss something if you both speak very quickly.'

'I'm sure you'll be able to pick out and record the vital matters,' Jake said calmly, his eyes roaming her face. The determinedly clinical air was at odds with what he had expected.

'I'm sure I shall.'

The dining room was busy with tourists and businessmen. As soon as they found a table. Leigh pulled out the advertising leaflets and her notebook, and frantically began transcribing shorthand signs for the multitude of technical terms.

'Your efficiency is impressive,' Jake commented drily, raising a brow. 'I suppose if you're determined to be businesslike I'd better start work too.' He opened his briefcase and pulled out a sheaf of papers, scanning them rapidly before selecting one that demanded his concentration throughout breakfast.

Leigh allowed herself a quick glance at him as they finished their coffee, and was disconcerted to discover he was studying her, his eyes warm with amusement. It was obvious he thought she was acting out a role—that of the super-cool secretary, and for the time being he was content to play along. She had a few hours' grace, at least until Jake's business with Jimmy Tay had been transacted. Those hours must be used to bolster up her strategy, for eventually Jake would demand that they resume their former intimacy, she was sure of that. Jake was no fool, he wouldn't be easily fobbed off with excuses. She regretted now she had told him so insistently that she had never allowed another man to touch her since Patrick's death. Well, she'd just have to dredge up a secret lover, or perhaps even two, who were waiting for her back home. The more Leigh turned the idea over in her mind, the more it suited her purpose. If she

played her cards right perhaps she could convince Jake
that he was totally unimportant to her, just another
casual relationship, though it was doubtful he'd be
pleased to discover she was dismissing him as a one-
night stand.

'Time to go,' he announced, taking a last swig of
coffee and shoving his papers back into his briefcase.

As they walked along the bustling street towards the
Tay building she could sense his gradual withdrawal.
He never noticed the sun playing on the deep waters of
Victoria Harbour, or the crush of people. Jake St John,
high-powered business tycoon, was taking control, and
Leigh released a sigh of relief. For the present she was
safe. By the time their arrival was announced, and
Jimmy Tay came forward across his office floor to greet
them, Jake was concentrating on one thing only—the
contract.

Jimmy was a short, dapper young Chinese with a
dashing dress sense. He was all in white—white suit,
white shirt, white shoes. His black hair was greased back
like a bowling ball, and the only touch of colour in his
outfit was a wide tie of blood red. He pumped Leigh's
hand up and down for longer than was strictly necessary, and treated her to a wide smile of white and gold
teeth. Jake introduced her briefly as Mrs Nicholas, his
temporary secretary, and Jimmy accepted the description without comment. After offering cool drinks, which
they both refused, he provided comfortable leather
chairs and sat himself down behind a large rosewood
desk to face them.

'And how is my old friend Rory Milwain?' he
queried.

'Fine.' Jake's reply was brief, as he bent down to re-
trieve his papers from his briefcase.

'I hope he hasn't forgotten me?' Jimmy slipped a sly
wink at Leigh, who sat on Jake's left, slightly behind his
line of vision.

'No, no,' she assured him with a bright smile which
she hoped indicated a promise of Rory's gift. She wasn't
sure whether the Chinese knew she would be delivering

the wallet. Possibly Rory had already advised him by telephone. However, Jimmy appeared satisfied with her reply, for he winked again, a slow, meaningful gesture which said a thousand words. Then, smiling broadly, he put two plump hands flat on his desk and assumed a businesslike stance which was Hollywood-inspired. Leigh took out her notebook.

'Now then, Mr St John, shall we recap over the terms your company is prepared to offer? Personally I feel it unnecessary, after all I have dealt with Mr Milwain throughout, but my father was anxious you should have a final say in the matter before we both put our names to the contract.'

Leigh's pencil began to fly along the lines of the pad. The meeting had begun. Two hours later she was weary; her fingers were cramped and aching, and her brain battered with an increasing flood of words and figures which had been tossed between the two men. It was as though she had tunnel vision, and at the end of the tunnel were plain blue lines on white paper bearing a multitude of squiggles. As Jimmy terminated the conversation she leafed through the pages. Nearly three-quarters of the pad was full. This afternoon she would begin deciphering it all; she hoped it made sense! At times the interchange had been feverish and she'd been stretched to the limit to keep up with the flow of words. With an inaudible sigh she closed the book and slipped it into the folder.

'I'll leave the contract with you.' Jake laid the prepared document in its beige cover on Jimmy's desk.

'If you return at four we'll sign on the dotted line,' the young Chinese assured him. 'My father will be present.'

Jake smiled. 'I look forward to that.'

Jimmy put out his hand and gave Leigh such a hearty handshake that she winced. Again the gold-plated smile flashed on. It was with a lightheaded feeling of relief that she emerged into the hot sunshine. Jake apparently felt the same, for he gave a big sigh and smiled at her.

'Thanks,' he squeezed her arm, 'you were great! I

don't know how you managed to keep going. The meeting went well, I don't foresee any problems now. We managed to agree on everything.'

'I'll start typing out a rough draft this afternoon,' Leigh told him. 'Can you rustle up a typewriter from somewhere?'

'That's already been arranged. The hotel should have installed one in your room.'

'You think of everything.' Her admiration was genuine.

'Naturally.' He raised his eyebrows and grinned.

After a speedy lunch they returned to their respective rooms. The meal had passed easily. Jake still had half his mind on business, and it had been simple for Leigh to keep the conversation ticking along on purely impersonal matters. Jake's time before their return to the Tay building was carefully apportioned. He had already booked a series of telephone calls to various parts of South-East Asia, chasing orders and discussing various ventures.

'I'll be tied up for a couple of hours, I imagine,' he told her as they went their separate ways, 'but I'll give you a knock around three-thirty and we can have a cup of tea together before the final session with the Tays.'

Leigh tossed a casual assent over her shoulder and went into her bedroom. Her eyes widened dramatically when she saw the brand new electric typewriter which awaited her on the desk. She had expected a secondhand portable, not this gleaming monster. Jake's organisational powers were remarkable, which probably accounted for his high-flying career. Neat stacks of paper and carbon were beside the machine. She took out her notebook and started to type. The first few pages were easily transcribed, flowing fluidly into a cohesive report. Leigh was beginning to congratulate herself on her skill when she came to an abrupt halt. She wasn't so clever after all. The next passage didn't make any sense, even though she read it through a couple of times it was gobbledegook. Laboriously she transcribed it into longhand, substituting other words for the ones which didn't seem quite right, but still it was garbled. The meeting at this point had become rather aggressive, the words being shot backwards and forwards like gunfire. Leigh pushed at a tendril of hair which had escaped from the sleek pleat and sighed. The sensible solution would be to consult Jake, he'd be able to straighten out the passage. With luck she could catch him between phone calls.

She opened her bedroom door and was about to walk the short distance to his room when she noticed three uniformed police officers, a large European and two smaller Chinese, standing in the corridor outside Jake's room. Leigh hesitated, retreating into the doorway. Jake answered their knock and the bulky European began to speak in a booming voice which carried easily along the corridor to her.

'Good afternoon, sir. I'm Inspector Gregson, C.I.D. I'm sorry to trouble you, but I understand you are involved in a deal with James Tay, and we have reason to believe you may be trying to bribe him.'

'What!' Jake uttered an expletive.

'It's purely routine, sir,' the inspector hurried to assure him in placatory tones. 'We are duty bound to follow up all information received.'

'What information?' Jake demanded.

'A phone call, sir—anonymous. Obviously someone wishing to make trouble, but I'm afraid we shall have to search your room.'

Jake swore again.

'We all know corruption is a way of life in the East,' the policeman continued in his penetrating voice, 'but as you are doubtless aware, sir, even a special discount or personal gift is suspect.' A gaggle of tourists making their way along the corridor had stopped to listen.

'I'm well aware of the laws regarding bribery and corruption,' Jake snapped icily. 'I have nothing to hide. Please come in and look around.' The three policemen disappeared into Jake's room, closing the door behind them.

Leigh's heart raced. Hurriedly she went over to her suitcase and took out the packet Rory had given her.

From what she had overheard it was obvious the gift of the wallet could be construed as a bribe. She fingered it nervously, then, after a moment's hesitation, tore off the wrapping. The wallet was a beautiful piece of craftsmanship in shiny, rich brown crocodile skin. She opened it and gave a gasp. A wad of brand new five-hundred-dollar bills was neatly tucked into its folds. Leigh put a hand to her throat in confusion. Rory was bribing Jimmy Tay. What should she do? Pellmell thoughts charged through her head. She had to act, and quickly. With gritted teeth she strode determinedly into the bathroom. Seconds later she returned to the typewriter and started hitting at the keys with undue ferocity. The shorthand still didn't make sense, but she thrust it all down on paper in a nonsensical tirade. As her fingers flashed across the keyboard Leigh knew she was making errors, but she ignored them. Her entire attention was concentrated on expected sounds outside in the corridor. Eventually there came a brisk rap at the door.

Leigh swallowed hard. She was surprised that she managed to walk across the room to open the door, for her legs were like jelly. She gave a polite, questioning smile at the three policemen and Jake.

'Sorry to trouble you, miss,' the European officer boomed, stepping into the room. 'I understand you are this gentleman's secretary?' He jerked his head in Jake's direction.

'That's correct.'

'Would you mind if we had a look around your room? It won't take a minute.'

'Go ahead.'

Jake reached out and took her arm. 'Don't worry,' he said quietly, 'some lunatic has suggested we're about to bribe Jimmy Tay. The officers only want a quick look through your belongings.'

Leigh watched with a pounding heart as the policemen spread out, one going into the bathroom to examine her cosmetics, while another looked through the dresses hanging in the wardrobe. The large European concentrated on her case. 'What's this?' He picked up the torn brown paper packet.

'It's a wallet.'

'Yours?'

'No. It's a gift for Mr St John.' Jake's fingers tightened on her arm. She looked up at him, willing him to remain silent. His surprise was apparent in the sudden narrowing of his eyes.

'Oh yes?' The police inspector did not sound convinced. He pulled the wallet from its wrapping and opened it. The wallet was empty. 'Expensive,' he commented, his fingers rubbing the knobbly texture of the skin.

'Mr St John is a very good employer,' Leigh interspersed quickly, 'he deserves the best.'

'And gets it too,' the policeman drawled, turning from his scrutiny of the wallet to flick his eyes over them both in a gesture of cynical disbelief. Instinctively Leigh moved closer to Jake. He put an arm around her shoulders and held her tight, giving her comfort from his solid self-assurance, his calm command of the situation. The policeman pushed two fingers into the folds of the wallet and pulled out a small white card. Leigh's heart plummeted. In her haste she had failed to notice anything apart from the money. This must be some message, incriminating evidence. She tensed involuntarily and Jake's fingers caressed her arm, trying to soothe her.

A sly smile brightened up the inspector's face. 'Thank you for all those wonderful nights,' he read aloud. 'Here's hoping we'll get together on many other occasions in the future.' One of the Chinese officers sniggered, and Leigh flushed scarlet. The European slipped the note back into the wallet and dropped it back into her case.

'Sorry to have spoiled a nice surprise,' he said with a sniff. He looked her up and down. 'Wish I had a secretary like you to give me things!'

'Have you finished?' Jake said coldly, 'because if so I suggest you leave.'

'Just going, sir.' The policeman managed, with difficulty, to settle his features into a more appropriate expression. 'Sorry to have troubled you both. Obviously a hoax, but you understand we have to check everything out.'

'I understand.' Jake gave a terse nod of his head, making the thick hair fall across his brow.

'We'll leave you two alone now, sir,' the words brimmed with suggestiveness, 'we don't want to interrupt that beautiful working relationship.'

'Out!' Jake's face and his voice were grim. The inspector gave Leigh another quick flurry with his eyes, and then they were gone. Jake gripped her shoulders with harsh fingers for a few moments cautioning her to keep quiet. Together they listened. There was the distant boom of the policeman's voice along the corridor, and later the vague whirr of the lift.

Jake's hands tightened, bruising the flesh beneath the thin fabric of her cream suit. 'What the hell was that all about?' he demanded. 'That wallet was never meant for me.'

She took a deep breath and pushed his hands away to sit down heavily on the bed. 'It was from Rory, a gift for Jimmy Tay.'

'Stupid bastard!' Jake ground out. 'It's only a token gesture, but it could still have caused trouble.'

'It wasn't a token gesture, it was full of five-hundred-dollar notes.'

'Oh no!' Jake dragged a long-fingered hand across his brow. 'Where are they now? What did you do with the money?'

'I flushed it down the loo.'

His brows shot to his hairline.

'All of it,' Leigh continued shakily. 'Rory asked me to give the wallet to Jimmy, but I overheard the policeman talking to you. I realised the gift was a bribe, so I rushed in and opened it. Then I discovered the cash.' She looked up at him, her face stricken. 'I had no idea there was any money involved.'

'I know you hadn't.' He sat down and put a comforting arm around her. She leant against him, her body trembling in a nervous reaction.

'How much money was there?' Jake asked.

'I don't know. I didn't have time to count it, but it was all in new notes and it was a thick wad. I imagine it must have amounted to several thousand Hong Kong dollars.'

'Had you read the message?'

Leigh shook her head violently. 'No. I nearly died when the inspector produced it. Thank goodness it wasn't signed!'

'You realise that your reputation is ruined now?' His mouth twisted into a half smile, 'It'll be on police files that you and I are lovers.' His voice became low. 'Now I shall be forced to make an honest woman out of you.' His fingers strayed to her jaw, gently turning her to face him, and Leigh felt she would surely drown in those penetrating eyes.

'Who do you think telephoned the police?' she asked, smartly snapping the moment of intimacy. He raised his head, and she knew he was piqued by her subtle rejection.

'De Groot, I imagine,' he replied drily, standing up and moving away from her. 'He was probably out to make mischief—perhaps Jimmy is taking money from him, too. An anonymous phone call would cost nothing, but could possibly cause trouble for us. He'd be grateful for even a smatter of doubtful rumours about the honesty of Milwain International.' He thrust his hands deep into his trouser pockets and frowned. 'That policeman was hardly discreet, with that damn great voice of his. I'm sure the entire floor is aware we had a visit from the vice squad. I wouldn't be surprised if rumours weren't beginning to circulate right now.'

'But there was no bribe, the company is in the clear.'

'Thanks to you.' Jake's face darkened with anger. 'I'll annihilate Rory when I get back to Singapore! What on earth was he thinking about, putting you in danger like that? Leigh, you could have ended up in a prison cell!'

'And the company's reputation would have been in shreds.'

'The implications don't bear thinking about.' Jake

raked impatient fingers through his hair, pushing it back. He paced the room. 'I'll have to go and tell Tay Wong Chai what's happened. It's vital we're honest with each other. I've known him a long time, I owe it to him to come clean.'

'What about the contract?'

He made a harsh sound in the back of his throat. 'We can say goodbye to *that*. The thing that matters at this moment is emphasising the company's honesty. There'll be other contracts in the future, but only if we maintain our reputation for integrity.' He turned to her, thinking aloud. 'I'll telephone Frank and advise him of what's happened, then I'll fix tickets for the first flight out in the morning. The sooner I have you out of Hong Kong the better. I don't want you at risk.'

'I'll stay in my room and finish typing out the notes of the meeting.'

'Thanks.' He started pacing again. 'It's just a matter of how to approach old man Tay. Do you think Jimmy was aware the money was on its way?'

'I'm sure he was.'

Jake listened carefully as she explained Jimmy's satisfied reaction to his question that morning.

'Tay Wong Chai's going to be sorely disappointed. He's one of the few businessmen in the East who is entirely free from corruption. He brought his sons up to think likewise—or, at least, he thought he did.' Jake gave a bark of sardonic laughter. 'I don't know how long I'll be gone, so order yourself some dinner from room service when you feel hungry.' He bent over her, putting his hands on her upper arms. 'I'm so sorry about this unholy mess. I was planning for us to celebrate in style this evening, but now it's all been ruined.' He pulled her to her feet and held her close. 'I wanted us to be together, just the two of us.' The pressure of his lithe, muscular body against hers was indication enough of what Jake had had in mind. Leigh's heart thudded to a standstill.

'But now I'll be involved in this ugly business,' he continued wearily. 'I don't know how long it will take. Don't wait up for me.'

'I shan't,' she assured him in a weak voice, and he dropped a distracted kiss on her brow. Already he was computing the various modes of conduct which could be adopted to take the heat out of the situation. When he had gone Leigh heaved a tremulous sigh, and sat down again at the desk. It was an ill wind, she thought wryly. The only good thing to emerge from Rory's disastrous decision to sweeten Jimmy's palm was that Jake would be too busy to pursue his love-making.

By seven o'clock she had completed the first draft from her notes, and decided to take a break. She telephoned an order for a light meal to be sent up to her room, and when she had finished eating, returned again to the typewritten pages and checked them laboriously against the shorthand. There was still the one passage which refused to make sense, but out of so many pages it was only a minor defeat. Tiredly she clipped the sheets together and pushed them away in the folder. It had been an exhausting day, and now she was physically and mentally drained. Leigh yawned and slotted the 'Do Not Disturb' sign over the doorknob.

As she undressed she wondered how Jake was progressing. There had been no sound from his room, so presumably he was still involved in his confrontation with the Tay family. It could be a nasty meeting, she thought with a shudder. Jimmy Tay could easily deny everything, or offload the entire blame on to Rory, or even try to implicate Jake. A cold shiver of fear ran down her spine as she imagined Jimmy, coldbloodedly altering the truth. It was unfair that Jake alone had to deal with the accusations and bitterness. He had been completely innocent. It was Rory, safely back home in Singapore, who had caused this chaos. She lay awake until midnight, fretting over the dilemma, but eventually tiredness crept over her and she slept.

She woke early the next morning, and a quick look at her watch revealed that it was only seven o'clock. It was impossible to settle back and doze, her mind was too active, so she showered and dressed, and was fixing her face when the telephone rang.

'Jake here,' he told her quickly. 'Can you be ready to leave in half an hour? There's a flight for Singapore around nine. I want us to be on it.'

When she agreed he murmured a few comments of relieved thanks and put down the phone. Leigh rapidly completed her make-up, smoothing fern green shadow on to her eyelids, and adding a touch of mellow rose lip-gloss. The face she presented to the world was immaculate. Speedily she packed her suitcase, putting her handbag beside it on the bed. When she was ready and waiting she stood before the full-length mirror and idly examined her reflection. The khaki-coloured blouse and matching culottes fitted well, emphasising her neat waist and high breasts. She tugged at the auburn curtain of hair around her shoulders. She didn't *look* like a forward young woman at all, she decided, her mind returning, as it had done repeatedly, to her evening in Jake's arms. Indeed she looked surprisingly shy and restrained. Leigh blushed again as her thoughts travelled back to the heedless manner in which she had responded to his lovemaking. Their speedy return to Singapore meant there was no time for more sightseeing, but that didn't matter. It was a blessing that they were leaving Hong Kong. When she was back with the O'Briens she could discreetly retreat from Jake, and make sure they would not be alone together. Then there would no longer be any temptation—thank goodness.

The rushed car journey and race through the airport denied anything more than the briefest of conversation, and it was only when they were settled and the plane was heading southwards through the clouds that there was time to talk.

'What happened with the Tays?' Leigh enquired, sipping at a tumbler of fresh orange.

'Everything,' Jake revealed with a groan. 'It was after two when I eventually returned to the hotel. I was with Jimmy and his father for five hours. At first Jimmy denied any knowledge of the money, then he insinuated that Milwain International had always smoothed the way financially. Fortunately his father is a wily old bird, he soon put a stop to those lies.'

'You've known Tay Wong Chai for several years, haven't you?'

Jake nodded. 'He knows I'm honest. All I could do was tell him the facts. I'm head of the Singapore company and all the actions of its employees, even the Chairman's son, are ultimately my responsibility.' He sighed. 'Things became quite violent at one stage, with Jimmy threatening all kinds of retribution.' Leigh noticed the lines of strain on his face. His emotional resources had been drained by the stress of the meeting.

He leant back in his seat and closed his eyes wearily. 'However, after some pretty straight talking I forced Jimmy to admit he'd virtually held a gun at Rory's head by telling him he'd only secure the contract if Jimmy was handed a slice of the profits—in advance, of course. Rory must have been so desperate to close the deal that he agreed. I presume the cash was his own, that's something I'll have to check.' Jake opened his eyes, they were a corrosive gray. 'I'll crucify him for involving *you* in his underhand schemes!'

Leigh put her fingers on his wrist. 'I'm sure he never thought he was putting me at risk.' She could feel Jake's scarcely controlled fury.

'That's just it, *he doesn't think*. My God, he'll have to change his ways,' he threatened. 'His thoughtlessness is too dangerous. This isn't the first time he's landed himself in trouble, and it's invariably left to me to sort things out.'

'What happened before?' Leigh was intrigued.

'Forget it.' Jake wafted a hand in a vague gesture of denial.

'Will you have to tell Sir Clive about this episode?' she asked.

'What other option do I have?' A telltale nerve flicked in his jaw.

'Couldn't you reprimand Rory and leave it at that?'

'Are you making a plea on his behalf?' Jake asked scornfully.

Leigh flushed. 'No,' she denied, looking down at the empty glass in her hands. 'I suppose there's no other alternative?'

'None. I know it smacks of telling tales out of school, but Rory's action was criminal.' He turned to her, his tone suddenly gentle. 'I'm sorry. Don't worry about him too much, he'll grab some glory nonetheless. The deal is still on.'

Leigh's brows shot upwards.

'Even without his backhander our prices are highly competitive and delivery dates are excellent. The signed contract is in my briefcase now.'

'So Mr de Groot's malicious phone call didn't have the required effect?'

'We don't *know* it was de Groot,' Jake stressed, 'though I'd bet my last dollar it was.' He tugged at his tie. 'It's times like these when I wish I had a woman to go home to.' He gave her a searching glance. 'Someone to hold me close and tell me it doesn't matter, that business isn't all-important, which, of course, it isn't.' He stroked the back of her hand with a slow-moving finger. 'I wish I could say to hell with it all, and carry you off to some desert island where we could make love all day and all night.'

Leigh's throat was paralysed. She had been relaxed while Jake was talking about business, but now he was turning his thoughts to more personal matters, making her heart rampage around all over the place.

'I need a wife,' he informed her, glancing across from beneath his dark lashes.

She wondered, for a moment, if it was a proposal, but gulped away the thought. 'Once a businessman, always a businessman,' she said, with a forced lightness. 'Any wife of yours would always take second place to Milwain International.'

'*She would not.*' His eyes burned. 'I only work so hard because there's nothing else to do. If I'm at home in the evenings Benjy is in bed, and there's no one to discuss the day's events with. At least if I keep moving I give myself the illusion of living life to the full.' His tone was bitter.

'But Choo's there.'

He scanned her face as though suspecting a hidden insinuation, but decided there was none. 'She's not a great conversationalist. If she'd been with me on the plane today instead of you we'd have lapsed into silence long ago. She isn't very stimulating.'

Leigh arched her brows. 'And I am?' The second the question escaped her lips she knew he would take it the wrong way. Even to her own ears it had sounded as though she was flirting with him, but she hadn't meant it to be a sensual enquiry. Indeed she had been referring to her own particular brand of conversation, but Jake's mind obviously flashed back to their time in bed.

'My girl, yes,' he affirmed, as his fingertips traced an urgent pattern in her palm. 'You stimulate me so much I can hardly bear it!' He smiled, his eyes suddenly warm and relaxed. 'The other evening was wonderful, the ultimate in communication.' He brought her fingers to his lips and kissed them, then his face clouded. 'Damn Rory to hell for destroying our time together! I'm afraid things will be rather hot businesswise for a day or two until I clear this matter up, my love, but after that I'll push Milwain International to one side and concentrate on *us*.' His eyes held hers in a look of tenderness which Leigh found unbearable. She tried, desperately, to look away, to break the mood, but she was transfixed, made speechless and immobile by the look of love in his eyes, the love that she knew she must deny if she was to keep control of her life.

It was early afternoon when they landed at Changi Airport. As they emerged into the busy Arrivals Hall Jake's Malay driver pushed his way forward to greet them.

'Important letter, sir.' He held out a white envelope. Jake frowned, pausing to slit open the flap with his finger. His face paled visibly as he perused the enclosed note.

'Everything happens at once,' he complained.

'What's the matter?'

'It's Choo's baby. He's had a convulsion, and is in hospital. Choo will need me there, she's not very good at coping with difficulties.'

He handed Leigh's suitcase to the driver and picked up his own, then, with long strides, hurried them through the building, throwing words back over his shoulder. 'I'll drop off at the hospital first, and then the driver will take you home.'

Leigh struggled to keep pace. He seemed to have almost forgotten her existence with this additional worry, and scarcely said a word on the drive to the hospital. He stared blindly out of the window, his mind somewhere far away. Leigh examined him. Beneath his tan his face was drawn, and there were dark rings around his eyes. She remembered that he must have grabbed only a few hours' sleep before their flight, but even so she felt irrationally angered by his distraction. His deep involvement with Choo and her baby was apparent. With a brief, backward farewell he leapt from the car as it drew up outside the hospital, and within seconds had disappeared from sight through the swing doors.

'Mr O'Brien's, please,' Leigh told the driver, and leant back in her seat, telling herself she was being unfair. How could she possibly feel piqued by Jake's withdrawal when, in truth, she really wanted him to ignore her? It didn't make sense. Wearily she pushed back a loose tendril of hair. What a dramatic two days it had been!

Bridget pounced on her as soon as she arrived. 'What's happened, what's happened?' she demanded, waving her arms around in a firework display of flashing gems. 'Frank said you and Jake were coming home early and that Rory had been a naughty boy.'

Leigh swallowed hard before composing a reply. She knew it was imperative she answer prudently. Whether Frank wished to tell Bridget the full details of Rory's unwise gift or not was entirely up to him, but for the time being she must tread warily, and on no account must she even hint that the relationship between her and Jake had altered. 'Everything,' she said, with a decisive flourish. Bridget's eyes shone in anticipation. Her shameless curiosity was on full alert. She led Leigh to a sofa, sitting down beside her, head cocked to one side like a sparrow awaiting a juicy titbit.

'We went to Aberdeen, and Repulse Bay, and the Peak. Then there was a meeting with Jimmy Tay, and later some trouble caused by Rory.' Leigh scarcely drew breath as she rattled out the words. 'Jake had a long discussion with old Mr Tay, and this morning we took an early flight home. The weather was bright and sunny, and the hotel was good.'

Bridget's bright air of expectation faded a little.

'And now,' Leigh continued determinedly, 'Jake's gone straight to the hospital. Choo's baby has been ill and she needs him there.' She fingered the pearl drop at her neck. 'He seemed quite distraught when he heard the news.'

The older woman scanned her face. 'Well, he would, wouldn't he!' she retorted. 'Surely you've seen the baby. You've noticed.'

'Noticed what?'

'It's Eurasian, half Chinese, half English. The reason Jake is so worried is because the child is his son.'

CHAPTER SEVEN

THE words took Leigh's breath away, and she gazed at Bridget in astonishment. Never, for one moment, had she imagined Jake had fathered Choo's baby, indeed she had never given conscious thought to the matter. If anything she had presumed the child to be the result of some illicit love affair between Choo and a boy-friend in Indonesia. Now, Leigh realised with sickening awareness, everything slotted so neatly into place.

'Naturally it isn't common knowledge, but you must have noticed how Jake is very protective over her,' Bridget continued blithely, unaware of her guest's thundering apprehension. Leigh remembered his fury at Rory's unexpected arrival on the scene with Choo. Jake's reaction *had* seemed extreme, but the fact that the girl was the mother of his child put an entirely different slant on the situation.

'Why doesn't he marry her?' Leigh wondered aloud.

Bridget gave a worldly laugh, a laugh which sounded ugly and a little cruel to Leigh's ears. 'Because he's not stupid, that's why. Jake is a highly successful businessman, destined for much greater things, and he's a realist. A wife like Choo would be a millstone around his neck. She's basically a simple soul, superstitious and easily upset. Her English is poor and she makes little effort to improve it. Why should she bother? She's a beautiful girl.' Bridget sniffed. 'What Jake needs her for doesn't require conversation,' she added crudely.

'But he gives the impression of being a man who cares.' Leigh felt as though she was fighting through a web of secrets that repelled and yet, at the same time, fascinated her.

'He is,' the older woman confirmed. 'Don't be shocked because he doesn't intend to marry her, I'm sure Choo doesn't expect it. She'll be quite contented as

133

long as he provides her with enough money on which to live comfortably.'

'Supposing Jake found a woman he liked and wanted to get married?'

Bridget examined her manicured nails. 'He'd discreetly buy Choo a house and settle some money on her and the child. He's a wealthy man, he could easily afford it.'

'And what about his wife's reaction!' Leigh's voice was rising on a note of high indignation.

'If she had a halfpennyworth of sense she'd turn a blind eye. A wise woman would learn to accept the realities and compromise. The Chinese girl is no threat. She has no desire to move in high circles.'

'I'd never compromise. I'd never accept that my husband had a—concubine,' Leigh spat out contemptuously.

Bridget laid a restraining hand on her arm. 'Why on earth not? Jake doesn't love Choo, though I admit he's fond of her. I expect the baby was a mistake. It's only because he's a caring man, as you said, that he fulfils his responsibilities towards it. Surely that's to be commended? Most men would have fobbed the girl off with a few hundred pounds, whereas Jake must have spent thousands on its hospital treatment alone over the past few months.' Bridget raised her brows and laughed. 'Don't look so outraged! Face facts, Leigh. The world isn't perfect.'

'I don't expect it to be perfect,' she said miserably. 'It's just that I never imagined Jake was ...' she hesitated, 'like that.'

'He's a virile young man, with natural desires. You don't imagine he's lived like a monk for the past five years, do you?'

'No, but ...'

'No buts about it,' Bridget said firmly, 'he's behaved honourably. Most illegitimate Eurasian kids don't fare half as well as Choo's son.'

Leigh rose quickly to her feet, her distress evident in her drawn face. 'I'll go and change. I feel rather grubby after the journey.'

Bridget gave her an understanding smile and reached across to pat her hand. 'Don't allow Choo and her baby to soil your opinion of Jake. You must admit he doesn't shove his skeletons away in a cupboard, and besides, I think he fancies you.'

'Does he?' Leigh answered cryptically, and swung away to her room.

With unseeing eyes she stared out of the window, wishing desperately that Bridget had kept quiet. She didn't want to know about Jake's second son. Her head started to throb, and her eyes brightened with irrational unshed tears. What a complex man he was, she thought bitterly. His appraisal and action over Rory's attempted bribery had been so *right*. She had felt nothing but admiration for him, but now ... Her stomach muscles knotted in dismay. His refusal to marry Choo belittled him. Jake was selfish, utterly and irrevocably. She thought again about his role in Patrick's death. Then his demands had been self-centred, and now, in another way, his behaviour was just as egotistical with Choo. What right had he to consign the Chinese girl to a life without a proper husband, while he was free to make love to, or marry, whomsoever he pleased? No wonder he didn't like Rory. He was jealous of him! Jealous that Rory might care for Choo, though he himself didn't care enough to give his name to her child. Leigh began to unbutton her shirt. Bridget's revelation was distressing, but it made her realise that the sooner she was rid of all contact with Jake, the better.

She had a quick bath and changed into a yellow tee-shirt and brief gold satin jogging shorts. Then, thrusting light-soled flip-flop sandals on to her feet, she went through into the lounge.

'It looks like rain,' Bridget commented from her seat by the window, where she was busily working on a needlepoint cushion in a bright Bargello pattern of turquoises and rusts. 'Look, you can see it's already pouring down on some parts of Singapore.'

From their vantage point on the twenty-third floor

the view was magnificent. Leigh joined her, and gazed out across the island. Leaden stormclouds were shedding their load of tropical rain in the distance, though the sun continued to shine above the apartment block. Leigh was grateful Bridget's attention had been diverted, thus sparing further comment on Jake's unsavoury personal life.

'It's so localised you can never tell whether the rain will reach here or not,' Bridget continued. 'I've known it to be pouring down a few hundred yards away, but remain bone dry here. Good heavens!' Her hand flew to her mouth in agitation. 'Did you see that?' A jagged streak of brilliant white lightning had pierced the gun-metal grey of the sky. Before Leigh could speak there came a roll of deafening thunder that made the windows rattle.

'This is one of those times when I don't enjoy living up in the sky one little bit,' Bridget said worriedly. She shuddered as another spear of electricity ripped through the clouds. 'I'd better take all the electric plugs from their sockets, these tropical storms can be nasty.'

As she disappeared into the kitchen the telephone rang. Leigh lifted the receiver. The line was distorted, and there was an alarming crackle as another flash of lightning brightened the dark sky. She held the phone an inch or two away from her ear.

'Missy, missy, Choo here!' Leigh frowned, straining to hear the words amidst the interference on the line. The Chinese girl sounded almost hysterical. 'Me home now from hospital. Baby okay, but Benjy he gone!'

'Gone where?'

'Don't know,' Choo started crying. 'Gardener look after Benjy. He say he gone in jungle. Me very frightened—much rain. You come find Benjy.' There was another ear-piercing crackle, and Choo gasped and put down the phone.

'Who was that?' Bridget asked, her usually cheery face tense and pale.

'Choo—she thought she was speaking to you. She sounded very upset, apparently she's come home from

the hospital and can't find Benjy. The storm must be
close to Jake's house, the noise was deafening over the
phone.'

'Poor girl, she's even more frightened of thunder-
storms than I am.' Bridget cast a wary look out of the
window at the approaching clouds. 'I suppose I'd better
drive over there and see what's happened.'

'I'll go,' Leigh offered impetuously, 'I don't mind the
thunder.'

'That would be kind of you, my darlin',' Bridget
accepted the offer with alacrity and undisguised relief.
'Benjy's probably just hiding in the house somewhere.'

Leigh grabbed her handbag and went down in the
lift. A taxi was dropping off a passenger at the entrance
to the apartments, so she quickly commandeered it and
gave the address to the driver. Why hadn't Choo con-
tacted Jake? Perhaps he was still tied up at the hospital.
The girl hadn't made it clear whether the baby had
returned home with her, or was still under medical care.
It was all very confusing.

The bright sun faded, and as they pulled out on to
Bukit Timah Road, the main north-south carriageway,
large drops of rain began to splash on to the windscreen.
The Indian driver wound up his window and grimaced.
'Big rain,' he said, pointing to the storm drain in the
centre of the road. The drain was as deep and wide as
an English canal, and surged with fast-flowing murky
brown water. It began to pour. The driver switched the
windscreen wipers on to full, but was still hard pressed
to see his way through the driving rain. A sudden gust
of wind rocked the vehicle, sending a flurry of small
twigs and branches hurtling on to the road. Leigh
watched in dismay. The driver motored steadily along
in the middle of the carriageway, keeping clear of vast
black puddles which were creeping across the tarmac,
threatening to flood the road. The level of the storm
drain grew ominously higher. All the traffic had slowed
down drastically, hampered by the darkness and the
force of the storm. Leigh became increasingly edgy as
the minutes passed. Presumably if Benjy was not in the

house he had wandered off into the estate bordering Jake's garden. The land there was wild and overgrown, and could, she supposed, be classed as jungle. The estate was owned by an absentee landlord, a Malay sultan, who regarded it as an investment. He made little effort to cultivate the land, and the trees and bushes had been left to rampage thick and strong in the fertile humid heat of the tropics. Even the large house in the centre of the grounds had been allowed to go to rack and ruin.

After what seemed like hours, but was only twenty minutes according to her watch, they arrived at Jake's home. The minute the taxi braked beneath the covered porch the front door was jerked open and Choo emerged, her face pale and tear-stained, the baby perched on her hip. Leigh paid off the driver.

'Where Missy O'Brien?' Choo asked, puzzled.

'Missy O'Brien sent me,' Leigh told her firmly, putting an arm around the girl's thin shoulders. 'I'll go and look for Benjy.'

'Thank you, missy.' The baby was hitched up higher on to her slender hipbone with no ceremony at all. Leigh gave it a quick look. It looked like any other Chinese baby to her, with its black hair and slanting eyes. It certainly didn't resemble Jake.

'Have you searched the house thoroughly? You're sure Benjy is not indoors?'

'He not in house,' the girl said emphatically. 'He out in rain. Gardener tell me.' Her almond eyes filled with tears, and she sniffed. She wiped her nose with the back of her hand, and clung on to the baby with the other.

'Calm down,' Leigh said gently. 'Where is he likely to be?'

'In Sultan's house, missy. Sometimes he go through fence to big house. I tell him not safe, plenty snake, but still he go. Mister Jake he get very cross.'

'Why haven't you rung Jake?'

'Mister Jake bring me home, then he go office. I telephone Sunantha, but she say he not there. Soon as he arrive she tell him to come back home straight away.'

Lightning crackled close by, briefly illuminating the

house and garden with an eerie glow. Choo cringed and stepped back into the hall. 'You find Benjy, missy. Take this.' She thrust a large brown waxed paper umbrella into Leigh's hands.

'Telephone Sunantha again,' Leigh instructed. 'Tell her Mr Jake is to come home now.' She thrust the umbrella over her head and stepped out from the cover of the porch into the pouring rain. 'And put that baby down in his cot—you'll be upsetting him again, hauling him around like that!'

'Yes, missy.' Choo gave a wisp of a smile, then disappeared into the house as a rumble of thunder rolled overhead.

Leigh tightened her grip on the wooden handle of the umbrella. The rain reverberated off the waxed paper in a noisy staccato, only matched by the bounce of the water on the driveway. She set off. Within seconds her flimsy sandals were waterlogged, and as she stepped on to the grass she bent down and slipped them off, dangling them from one finger. She strode across the soft, wet garden, quickening her pace when she saw the hole in the fence. It lightened again and she gave an involuntary shudder. The gods were angry. The rain lashed at her bare legs like a badtempered whip, and the wind tossed her hair into her eyes. Her tee-shirt and shorts were quickly soaked and clung to her like damp, warm rags. Leigh scrambled through the hole in the fence and started to follow a muddy track through the undergrowth.

'Benjy, Benjy, where are you?' The gusty wind carried her voice away, reducing it to a thin quiver which was lost in the noisy concerto of the storm. There was no answer.

The downpour was quickly turning the track into a torrent, and she was conscious of mud spattering her legs as she hurried along.

'Benjy, Benjy!' She peered into the thick tangled undergrowth and remembered Choo had said something about snakes. An icy shiver brought goose pimples to her arms as she endeavoured to convince herself it was

highly unlikely a snake would be slithering along in this
weather. There was another finger of lightning, and
Leigh swallowed hard, her heart thumping in her chest
as she broke into a run. Again the thunder rattled
around. It was too close for comfort. A hard, choking
lump of fear stuck in her throat. It was true she wasn't
normally afraid of thunder, but to be out in a tropical
storm while the gods hurled their abuse was little short
of foolhardy.

'Benjy, where are you?'

Another bang of thunder shook the earth, and her
senses screamed. If only she could reach the house,
surely Benjy would be there, and he'd be terrified, poor
little boy. She was halfway terrified herself. The wind
pulled at the umbrella, but she hung on, stumbling along
the muddy track as quickly as she could. The vegetation
on either side was robust and treacherous. She tripped,
her leg scraping against a tree stump in an undignified
scramble to remain on her feet. She was trembling.
Resolutely she clutched the brolly, and set off again at a
slower pace. 'More haste, less speed,' she muttered. The
wind hurtled around. There was a high-pitched scream,
and Leigh stopped in her tracks, her head whipping
round in the direction of the noise. Two solemn eyes
regarding her from the branch of a tree. She gave a
burst of weak laughter that had its roots in hysteria.
The onlooker was a little grey monkey.

'Pull yourself together, girl,' she told herself firmly.
At last she saw the house, fifty yards away through the
rain. She ran quickly across the broken tarmac and into
the building. It was only a shell, the doors and windows
had disappeared years ago, leaving huge gaping holes
through which the wind and rain lashed like wet
spears. The concrete floor was littered with debris, but
at least the roof was intact. Leigh marched to the centre
of the ground floor where it was dry, and put down the
umbrella.

'Benjy, Benjy, it's Leigh! Where are you?' She cupped
her hands to her mouth and shouted, but the only reply
was the incessant thrum of the rain. Leigh looked about

her. She was standing in what must have been a grand reception room, for thick white pillars supported the ceiling, and to the left was a wide wooden staircase which must have been magnificent when it was new, many years ago. Now it was broken and insecure, but with tentative steps she began to climb it, shouting as she went. When she reached the fifth stair there was an alarming creak. She tested her weight on it, and stepped back quickly as the wood splintered and fell away.

'Benjy, Benjy!' She raised her head and yelled frantically up the stairs.

'Leigh!'

The sudden sound of her name came from behind her, and she spun round. Jake was running through the rain into the house.

'You stupid girl!' he hurled, as he reached the bottom of the stairs, 'have you no sense! What the hell do you think you're doing, running around in this weather? You could have been killed!' He looked ready to kill her himself, his chest rising and falling in his fury. His lips were a thin, savage line across his face, and his eyes burned with some violent emotion that seemed to be threatening to engulf him entirely. His pale grey trousers were covered in mud from the knees down, and his shirt was soaked.

She glared at him, her eyes like circles of cold steel. 'I'm looking for *your* son,' she snapped. She was tempted to add, 'Your elder one,' but she didn't.

'Benjy is at home.' Jake's voice was heavy with the ferocity of his anger.

'Choo said he was here!'

'He was sheltering from the rain in the garage. The door was closed, nobody could see him.' Jake attempted to push back his hair which was plastered wetly across his brow, but without success. It stuck stubbornly in a straight dark fringe above his thickly lashed eyes. Droplets of rain coursed down his face, and Leigh watched in fascination as one drop started at his hairline and trickled slowly down his tense jaw and throat to lose itself in the wet cotton of his collar. A limp dark tie hung from his neck.

'Why didn't you wait until I came home?' he demanded, still panting from his run.

'I had no idea how long you would be,' she said reasonably, 'and I thought Benjy would be scared to death.'

'So you scare me half to death,' he said tersely, his jaw moving in agitation.

'I'm sorry.'

'No, no,' he was immediately contrite. 'It's I who should be sorry. I shouldn't shout at you. After all, you are on an errand of mercy.' He lifted a self-deprecating brow. His anger had disappeared. 'You've scraped your leg.' He pointed to a thin trickle of blood running among the pale brown mud on her knee.

'It doesn't hurt.'

There was a rumble of thunder, and Leigh looked out apprehensively at the storm which showed no sign of abating.

'We'll give it half an hour,' said Jake. 'Surely it will have lessened by then, these tropical storms are usually short and sharp.'

'Shouldn't we get back to Choo?'

For some reason Leigh sensed a change in his mood, though she could never have defined it. He was looking at her with an almost glazed expression.

'We'll wait until it stops raining,' he said abstractedly, 'she won't come to any harm.'

'What about the baby?' Her question was a touch tart, but Jake didn't seem to notice.

'He's okay at the moment, but the doctor says he could have more convulsions, apparently he's prone to them. He should grow out of them as he gets older. Normally they wouldn't be too serious, but as he has a heart defect he needs special care. Apparently he inherited the weakness.'

'Did Benjy have convulsions when he was a baby?'

Jake gave her a strange look. 'No. Why?'

She shrugged. 'I just wondered.'

'What has Bridget been telling you?' he demanded.

He took a step closer and grabbed her arm, pulling her down off the staircase until he towered over her. He shook her roughly, his wet hand sliding across her flesh in a touch which was at once frightening and sensual.

'Nothing,' Leigh protested.

'Are you sure?'

Frantically she nodded her head, keeping silent. Jake's fingers tightened and he pulled her hard against him until she could feel the muscular leanness of his long body against hers. His breath was hot on her cheek.

'I presume you're not on the pill?' The question took her unawares. For a moment she stared blankly up at him, then the shock of realisation hit her. Jake laughed softly at her expression. 'Don't look so incredulous, my beautiful girl. It's quite possible our night of love will produce a child.'

'Oh, Jake!' The words were a combination of awe and dismay.

'Don't tell me you'd never thought of it before?' He bent his head and kissed her deeply, his plundering mouth demanding, and eventually receiving her answering desire.

'You really are a delightful mixture,' he muttered against her hair. 'You're the hottest creature I've ever known in bed, and yet, at times, you're so naïve it's unbelievable.' His lips moved across her brow, making the blood surge like molten gold through her veins.

'I'm not hot,' she denied uncertainly, as his fingertips resumed their erotic tattoo.

'You're very hot,' he repeated firmly. 'Just look at you now!' His breathing had quickened and she felt the heavy rise and fall of his chest against her.

'What do you mean?'

His glance fell to the wet tee-shirt which was clinging to her, shamelessly outlining her breasts with their taut pinnacles. 'Do I have to spell it out for you?' He pulled the damp cotton from her chest. 'If you ever decide to pose for *Penthouse* magazine I guarantee you'll be Pet of the Year.' His voice grew throaty. 'I want to make love to you again, my darling, and very soon.'

'No.' Her reply was meaningless, for as his fingers caressed the silken skin of her breasts she gave a muffled sob and buried her face against his wide shoulder.

'Don't disappear behind that barrier again,' he said thickly, his fingers teasing the sensitive pinnacles, creating waves of exquisite pleasure that made her arch against him, her body eager and straining. She threaded her arms around his neck and pulled his mouth down to hers, drinking in his desire.

'You're beautiful,' he murmured huskily, his touch relentlessly arousing her until she lost all awareness of time and place, and thought she would faint with pleasure. He paused for a moment to pull at his shirt, then his muscular naked chest was against her. He cast a wry glance at the debris-strewn floor. 'Oh darling,' he moaned, 'do you think we could possibly make love standing up?'

She pressed closer against him, her feverish body giving him its own reply.

'Tell me that you want me, Leigh,' Jake insisted into her throat.

She trembled as his mouth slurred across her skin, making a ruthless path to the swell of her breasts.

'Say it.'

She tried to assemble a modicum of self-control. 'No.' The word was a whisper. His lips were burning into her flesh, making the blood pound in her ears. The sensual journey across her skin continued until his mouth closed over her breast, sending such a delirious shaft of need through her body that she moaned his name aloud.

'Say it,' he muttered brokenly, his tongue working its way from one rosy peak to the other.

'I want you.' The answer rested on an unbidden sigh of desire.

His hands moved slowly down to the satin shorts at her hips. 'And tell me that you'll marry me, my darling, as soon as possible. I want you with me, living in my house, loving me.'

'No!' This time her reply was loud and defiant. Abruptly she twisted from his arms with furious strength, pulling down her tee-shirt across her traitorous breasts and standing back to face him, her expression fierce.

'Why not? I don't understand.' Jake drew a harsh breath, his powerful body quivering with emotion. The glittering gray eyes that probed hers demanded an explanation.

'I can never marry you.' The words were so quietly spoken he was forced to bend his head to catch them. Jake rubbed the back of his neck, torn between exasperation and bewilderment.

'I love you, and you love me,' he said patiently in a low voice. 'Perhaps I'm rushing things, but what's the point in waiting? I'm thirty-four, I'm old enough to know what I want—you. Surely you don't require the whole courting bit with flowers and chocolates and visits to the cinema, do you? It seems a little late for that now.'

Leigh's throat was paralysed with confusion. She stared at him with wide, stricken eyes, but saw only Choo—Choo and the baby. Perhaps Jake was right, perhaps she did love him, but even so marriage must be an impossibility. A more sophisticated woman might snap her fingers at the fact that Jake had a love-child, but she knew she couldn't. The knowledge of Choo would always be at the back of her mind. Jake had treated the girl wrongly in her eyes, and she knew the fact would grow like a cancer over the years to stultify their relationship.

'I don't love you,' she told him in a shaking voice, turning her head away, refusing to meet his eyes.

Jake swore under his breath. 'For heaven's sake, Leigh, you proved conclusively the other night just how strongly you felt about me.'

'Oh, that,' she gave a dismissive flick of her fingers and carried on quickly, the words tumbling out in a desperate attempt to appear casual. 'You don't imagine that meant anything? I'm a modern girl. If I want to sleep with someone I do, but I don't regard it as a prelude to anything more serious.' She gave a shaky laugh.

'There have been other men as well as you. What happened in Hong Kong was lust, pure and simple.'

'You don't expect me to believe that, do you?' he demanded roughly, his face darkening with anger. 'You're not promiscuous. You're a one-man woman, I know that. With you it's all or nothing, you wouldn't settle for an affair. You gave yourself to Patrick, and now you've given yourself to me.' He thrust out an angry hand and grabbed her hair. 'Don't play around,' he threatened. 'Don't think you can dart back behind that protective shield of yours. You know as well as I do you would never have slept with me if you didn't care for me deeply.' His fist tightened in her hair. 'Would you?' he insisted, dragging her towards him with such force that tears sprang to her eyes.

'Let me go!'

'Not until you stop telling lies.' His voice softened into a careful menace that sent a cold chill down her spine. 'You've never made love to any other men, have you, my beautiful girl?'

Her scalp throbbed with pain as he gave a sudden yank. 'No!' She flung the word at him, and felt like adding, 'So there,' like a belligerent child.

'And you do love me.'

'I might,' she muttered ungraciously.

'Thank you,' he said silkily, with a sardonic twitch of his brow. 'At last we appear to be getting somewhere.'

She closed her eyes. 'Let me go, please, Jake.' She was on the brink of sobbing out loud. 'Let me go!' she twisted furiously.

'Okay.' The release was so abrupt she staggered back. Jake reached out and put his hands on her upper arms, pulling her closer, mesmerising her by the forceful look in his eyes. 'Cut out the pretences, Leigh,' he ordered, 'tell me the real reason why you won't marry me.'

She gazed at him, trying desperately to form the phrases, to tell him she knew Choo was his mistress, but somehow the words stuck in her throat. Even to herself the accusation sounded melodramatic, and she knew he would consider she was making a great fuss over nothing. Jake was a man of the world, his attitude would be the same as Bridget's. He'd explain it away, persuade her it didn't matter, *but it did*. His eyes were hardening with impatience as she stood mute before him, pinned like a butterfly on a board.

'I'm waiting, Leigh,' he said in a voice that was too gentle.

She took a deep shuddering breath, and then, although it was unjust, although it wasn't the real reason at all, she heard herself saying, 'You killed Patrick.'

'Don't accuse me of that again,' he said angrily in a loud voice. 'Use your common sense.'

'You sent him to Kuantan,' she said in a small voice.

His hard fingers bit deep into the soft flesh of her arms. 'He went against my wishes,' he said from between gritted teeth. 'He was weak from the virus, I told him to cancel the visit.'

Leigh stared at him in open surprise.

'Ask Frank,' Jake said tersely, 'he'll confirm what I've said. Patrick was worried we'd miss the business if he didn't make the journey. A new civil engineering site was opening up, and he reckoned if he obtained the business for the first stage of the scheme other orders would follow.' He gave a bark of grim laughter. 'He was right. We've had over two million dollars' worth of business from them.'

Leigh gazed out at the pouring rain, recognising the honesty of Jake's words. She had been so busy hating him in the past she had never stopped to consider she might have got things wrong. Now it all began to make sense.

'I told him that if he insisted on going he must spend the night at a hotel,' Jake continued. 'Ten hours' driving in one day was too much for any man, let alone one who was unwell. The only reason he decided to motor home that night was because he wanted to be with you.'

Leigh raised her head sharply, narrowing her eyes. The impact of his words hit her like a blow to the body, and she gasped. 'So you blame me! You say it was my fault.' Her voice was harsh with pain.

'No, no. You've got it wrong, I don't blame you in the slightest,' he assured her, shaking her arm gently in a vain attempt to calm her. 'It wasn't a situation where anyone was to blame. It was an accident. I told you before, there could have been a number of reasons why the car crashed.'

Leigh swayed, bemused by the pressure of a thousand savage thoughts that rattled around her brain. Jake had accused *her* of killing Patrick! Scalding tears blinded her eyes as she violently pushed her way past him, out into the storm. She ran. The only thing that mattered was to get away. Leigh could hardly see for the tears that smarted in her eyes as she dived into the undergrowth, oblivious of the driving rain, the rip of thorns against her legs, the wind-tossed branches that caught at her hair. The lightning flashed, closely followed by an earth-shaking bolt of thunder. Blindly she ran, fighting for breath. There was a pain in her chest like a scorching ball of fire. She didn't know where she was going, and didn't care. At the back of her mind she was conscious of Jake pounding along behind her, calling her name, telling her to stop. Desperately she increased her pace, then she was back on the path, the muddy water running over her bare feet, splashing up her legs.

She never noticed the root. It had been exposed by the force of the heavy rain, and lay like a rigid snake some inches above the ground. Her foot caught it in her flight, and she flung out her hands to save herself. As she fell there was a ripping sound as a vicious streak of lightning tore the sky apart. Pain, like a red-hot needle, seemed to pierce the top of her head, and then there was blackness.

Everyone had been so kind. The room was full of flowers—bright arrangements of carnations and chrysanthemums, orchids and flamingo flowers, all sent with good wishes for her speedy recovery from old friends, casual acquaintances and the office staff. Leigh moved fractiously in the hospital bed. Although she had been inundated with letters and telephone calls, there had been no contact with Jake, and he was the one person she desperately wanted to see. True, he had sent flowers, two dozen dark red rosebuds which were slowly opening, filling the room with their sweet fragrance, but the accompanying white card held no message, only his scrawled signature—Jake.

Red roses were for love. Surely that meant he didn't regard her too harshly, she persuaded herself. Leigh wrinkled her brow—or was it *white* ones? Jake probably didn't know either. She tossed her head. It was entirely possible he had merely asked Sunantha to arrange flowers for her, and the florist had just received a consignment of red roses. They didn't signify anything, they were merely a polite gesture. Wearily Leigh placed the card on the bedside locker and fidgeted with the stiff white bow at the neck of her nightgown. It was hospital issue and looked it, in plain white cotton with long sleeves and a high restricting collar. Bridget had suggested she buy her a prettier one, but she had refused. It didn't seem worthwhile. Tomorrow morning she was due to be discharged, and then it was only a matter of days before she flew back to England.

'Feeling fit this morning, Mrs Nicholas?' A Chinese doctor in a starched white coat poked his head round the door.

'I'm fine,' she smiled.

'How's that ankle? Have you been doing the exercises?'

She nodded. 'It's strong again. I can walk without any difficulty.' She slipped out of bed and took a few steps.

'That sprain saved your life,' he told her sternly, following her movements as she paraded before him. 'If you'd been any closer to the lightning strike you could have been killed.'

'I know.' Her face was subdued. He had already berated her severely for being out in the storm.

'You were fortunate someone was around to pick you up and bring you to hospital in double quick time. Their prompt action certainly enabled us to treat you promptly and thus lessen the degree of shock.' He picked up the chart from the rail at the bottom of her bed and examined it. 'You'll be going home tomorrow after only three days, that's a speedy return to normality. Still you're young and strong.' He looked her up and down as though she were a weight-lifter, and Leigh decided wryly that she probably looked like one, in the voluminous nightgown.

'How are all the bumps and bruises?'

'Healing nicely, no problem.'

He examined a graze on her arm. 'Good.' He gave a bleak nod of dismissal and strode from the room. It was obvious he had little time for foolish European women who chose to risk their lives by irresponsible behaviour.

Leigh plumped up the pillows and propped herself upright in the bed. His disapproval was entirely justified, she was well aware she had acted foolishly, in more ways than one. The accident had precipitated one thing—she was not pregnant, at least that was certain now, and she knew she should be thankful. Leigh gazed out of the window. Since the storm the weather had been exceptionally bright and sunny, as though nature was endeavouring to compensate for her lapse of bad temper. A warm breeze ruffled the folkweave curtains, and Leigh pushed up her sleeves, her eyes moving from the sky of cloudless blue to the bedroom. The table groaned with vases and baskets of flowers. The hospital was a private one and very luxurious; she had a brand new television set, and the room was attractive with tastefully decorated walls and a thick russet carpet. She sighed. She had been unwilling to enquire as to who was paying for her treatment—it had to be Jake. He would be fulfilling his responsibilities yet again, she thought peevishly, and yet he was only generous with his money, not his time. He had never troubled to visit her. He was probably sick to death of her by now, she thought unhappily.

It was a relief when Bridget arrived and jolted her out of her introspection.

'Hello, my darlin', how are you today?' Bridget asked, rushing forward to kiss her cheek before producing an array of goodies from an immense straw shopping basket. Everything was set down on the bedspread for Leigh's approval. There were bunches of grapes, tissues, a bottle of tonic wine, oranges, a pineapple, three magazines, and a greeny-yellow papaya. 'There,' said Bridget with a satisfied smile, 'that should keep you going until tomorrow.'

Leigh grinned. There was no chance of her devouring the mound, which was already threatening to spill over on to the floor. 'You're very kind.'

'No bother,' Bridget beamed, pulling up a chair. 'I met the doctor in the corridor, he says you're fighting fit again—ankle nicely healed, shock cured, all those grazes attended to.' She leaned over and patted the girl's hand, then turned to survey the table of flowers. 'What a lovely display, who sent the roses?'

'Jake.'

'It was lucky he was there to rescue you. He caught some of the impact of the blast himself, and had to have a day in bed to recover, on doctor's orders.' Bridget laughed. 'You can imagine how furious he was! He doesn't like to have time off work.'

'Is he recovered now?' Leigh asked in a small voice.

'He's fine.' Bridget adjusted the heavy shell necklace at her throat. 'He played hell with Choo for sending you off on a wild goose chase.'

Leigh kept silent. From the little Bridget had said it was apparent Jake had merely told her they had both been searching for Benjy and had been near the tree when the lightning struck. She was grateful for his discretion. Colour flooded her face as she recalled her rash accusation and subsequent flight. Since then, she thought with a sigh, there had been plenty of time for self-analysis, plenty of time to realise her mistakes.

'Is Jake still away?' She struggled to appear offhand, but to her own ears the question sounded loaded with importance.

Bridget nodded, the stiffly set auburn curls vibrating like coils of wire. 'He shot off to Japan, for some reason.' She leant closer to Leigh. 'Has Rory been in to see you?'

'He was here yesterday,' Leigh confirmed.

Rory had entered the room sheepishly, like a school-boy who had accidentally broken a window. Initially he had been full of remorse over the Tay incident, and had offered abject apologies, apologies that were quickly dissipated in the light of her assurance that no harm had been done. Leigh had been left with an uncomfortable feeling that morally Rory didn't regret his action at all, because fundamentally he didn't see anything wrong in it. As they talked it became clear that his real regret was that the bribe had been discovered and that he, personally, was out of pocket by several thousand dollars.

'What a waste,' he had said ruefully. 'I could have used that cash to buy myself a sailing dinghy.'

Leigh had bit back an angry 'It serves you right,' for the retort would have been lost on him. Rory blamed the circumstances, not himself. He was deceiving himself, as she had deceived herself over Patrick's death, conveniently offloading the blame on to Jake and never considering her own role in the matter.

The longer Rory had chatted, the more she realised that any chance of a relationship developing between them had been reduced to zero. When he left she had felt relieved, and her thoughts had returned again to Jake as they had done incessantly throughout her time in hospital.

Bridget left her bedside to examine the cards accompanying the flowers, commenting on everyone's thoughtfulness and choice of blooms.

Leigh fiddled with her collar. 'I expect Jake will be home at the weekend.' Again she tried to keep the comment light, but obviously it didn't quite come off, for Bridget turned to her, an interested light in her eye.

'I imagine so. Why? Do you want to see him?'

'Not particularly,' Leigh replied airily, 'but I would like to thank him for his kindness.'

When Bridget departed she pushed herself down in the bed and closed her eyes. She wanted to see Jake

again and apologise, to tell him she had ceased to blame
him for Patrick's death, that it had just been an excuse.
It was only fair that she be honest and tell him the
truth—that Choo was the real reason why she wouldn't
marry him. Leigh gave a muffled sob. She loved Jake. It
was easy to admit it to herself now, but he must never
know how strongly she felt, for then he would insist
they marry, and that was impossible. It would only bring
pain. It was Choo he should marry, not her.

For the hundredth time that morning she wished she
was the kind of woman who would be unconcerned
about Jake's refusal to act decently with Choo, but she
wasn't. I'm too respectable, she thought unhappily, too
hidebound by the social norms and etiquette of present-
day society. Mistresses and children born out of wedlock
might be acceptable amongst film stars and the jet set,
but for ordinary people, like her, they represented an
uncaring attitude, where true love and loyalty played
little part. She would be relinquishing a vital part of her
character if she allowed her personal convictions to be
conveniently pushed aside. Deep down she knew she
would come to despise herself, and Jake—and yet, she
persuaded herself, there was really no reason at all why
their marriage shouldn't be a success. If they lived in
England then Choo and the baby would be far away on
the other side of the world, and surely she could train
herself to forget their existence.

She shrugged. The matter was hypothetical now,
anyway. Jake's absence was indication enough that he
wanted no more to do with her. She couldn't blame
him, and yet, despite his attitude, she still needed to
apologise to him. She must make amends, then go home
and never see him again. She reached for the tissues and
blew her nose noisily.

A tiny Chinese nurse came into the room. 'There's a
gentleman to see you,' she said. 'Very impressive, very
big. Shall I send him in?'

Leigh's heart somersaulted wildly. It must be Jake.
Now she would have a chance to explain her feelings.
She would do it tactfully, point out that everyone was

entitled to his own view, that she wasn't condemning him. Indeed, as Bridget had pointed out, Jake had acted kindly as far as things went. She sighed. The gap between Jake's code of ethics and her own was just too great, it could never be bridged.

Quickly she tossed the tissue into the waste paper basket and combed the auburn curls that tumbled over her shoulders. 'Please ask him to come in.'

Then she sat back and waited.

CHAPTER EIGHT

THE man was impressive and he was big, but he was not Jake. Leigh's spirits dropped with a thud, and she hoped her face didn't reflect her disappointment. The man was elderly—no, old, she decided brutally, but an upright military bearing belied his age at first glance. He had silver hair and a huge R.A.F. style moustache that festooned his upper lip like a Christmas tree decoration, ending, as it did, in two carefully tended twirls. He was resplendent in an expensively tailored black suit and brilliant white shirt. His tie seemed exclusive—probably he was an old boy of some élite public school, and a heavy chain in what could only be gold stretched across his portly frame from one side of his waistcoat to the other. He carried with him an aura of wealth and good breeding. 'My dear,' he beamed, striding forward to give her a powerful handshake, 'I've heard so much about you over the past couple of days I feel I know you already.'

Leigh gazed at him wide-eyed.

'I'm Clive Milwain,' he explained, sitting himself firmly down on the chair at her bedside. Leigh examined his face. Now he had introduced himself it was easy to detect the family resemblance, for his merry brown eyes had been handed down to Rory, and he had the same easy smile.

'It's nice to meet you, Sir Clive,' she began a trifle nervously, for it was the first time she had met anyone with a title.

'Delete the Sir,' he grinned, 'call me Clive.'

'Clive,' she repeated, in such a tentative voice that he laughed, and Leigh found herself laughing with him.

'I've come to apologise,' he said, the dancing eyes

155

becoming serious. 'You've been subjected to quite a holiday, young lady, haven't you? First police interrogation, and now being hospitalised.'

'I'm fine now,' she assured him quickly.

'Good, good. I know Rory has asked your forgiveness over the wallet affair, but I too wish to add my humble apologies.' He passed a huge wrinkled hand across his forehead. 'My son has been severely reprimanded. He's not a bad fellow at heart, but he's impetuous. I'm convinced he didn't intend to put you at risk, he just didn't think of the consequences. However, he's fully aware of his errors now, I hope.' He raised two heavy silver brows. 'It'll be a long time before he takes any chances again.'

'At least he secured the contract,' Leigh's soft heart made her add in justification.

The old man nodded. 'Thanks to Jake's expert handling of the matter.' He tugged at one twirl of his moustache. 'That's quite a flourish to finish on. He's already begun his final tour of the area.'

'His final tour?' she echoed, glancing across at the roses, her brow wrinkled. So Jake had decided to leave Milwain International immediately, he must have given his resignation to Sir Clive while she was in hospital.

'He'll relinquish his duties in Singapore at the end of next month,' Sir Clive confirmed.

'It will be a great wrench for him to leave Milwain International,' she said, fingering the cuff of her gown.

Sir Clive regarded her with puzzled eyes. 'He's not leaving the company.'

'He's not?' Leigh's voice rose on a note of surprise.

'Indeed no. He's taking over from me, as Chairman. He'll be based in London, it'll be easier for him there, with that boy of his. He won't have to travel so much.'

'I thought Rory was going to be Chairman,' Leigh said.

'So did he,' Sir Clive's reply was cryptic. 'I admit at one time I did harbour the hope that he'd fill my place, but over the years it's become increasingly clear he's not suited to the world of commerce. This unfortunate business in Hong Kong has merely served to reinforce my opinion.'

'Is he disappointed?'

Sir Clive pursed his lips thoughtfully. 'I don't think so, not deep down. Initially it was a blow to his pride, but he seems to have accepted it. I suspect at heart he's relieved—he's always found the pressures of Milwain International a little hard to handle.' He gave a snort of wry laughter. 'Already he's talking of opening a sports centre in Bali. His grandfather left him some shares in the company which I've suggested he sell to Jake. He should be able to afford quite a nice little spread, and who knows, he might turn it into a success.'

'I hope he does,' Leigh said earnestly.

'Thank you, my dear. My only fear is that he might spend most of his time sampling the sports himself.' Sir Clive shrugged his shoulders. 'Let's face it, Rory hasn't much ambition. I suppose you can't really blame him, everything has always been handed to him on a plate, he's never had to struggle or know what it is to work hard. I can't expect him to change his spots now.'

'Everybody likes him,' Leigh said with a smile. 'He has a charming personality.'

'Yes, he has,' the old man acknowledged. 'I suppose I should be thankful for that.'

They both looked up as a nurse knocked at the door and sidled in bearing a tray with a pot of tea, lemon slices, and a plate of biscuits. As they drank their tea and chatted Leigh completely forgot he was titled, and old enough to be her grandfather. Indeed, his flexible outlook and up-to-the-minute jokes totally belied his years, and she soon discovered he was as easy to respond to as Rory. The old man was delighted to be in her company, and flirted outrageously. He demolished all the chocolate biscuits, popping them into his mouth, one after another, with great gusto. 'Supposed to be counting calories,' he smiled, patting his ample stomach. 'But never mind. My wife will have to put up with an extra pound or two of me—more to love!' He gave a broad wink. 'I'm off to Australia tomorrow to look at our factory there, and I understand they make the most delicious pavlovas, dripping with fresh cream. Oh dear!' There was a mock groan of despair.

Leigh giggled.

'Don't know how you young folk keep so trim,' he continued, pouring them both second cups of tea. 'There's not an ounce to spare on either Rory or Jake, or you, too, I'll be bound, beneath that huge nightie of yours.' He took a sip of tea. 'It's about time Jake was married again.' He gave her a keen glance. 'He'll need a wife to help him with all the socialising he'll be expected to do as Chairman, and to set up home for him in London.'

'I expect Choo will look after his house,' Leigh said flatly, her jaw tightening a fraction.

Sir Clive gave a loud bellow of laughter. 'Come now, young lady, you don't seriously expect him to take that little Chinese slip of a girl with him, do you? Good heavens, she'd be completely out of her depth in London! For a start, her grasp of the English language is pretty pathetic.'

'She could learn,' Leigh said defiantly.

'Out of the question,' Sir Clive said firmly with a dismissive wave of the hand. 'Jake needs a woman who's much more than a servant. He needs a partner. He's a strong character, it would have to be someone with a bit of spirit.' He winked. 'I reckon someone young and pretty would be just the ticket.'

Leigh blushed.

When he left she wandered around the bedroom, smelling the flowers, re-reading her cards. Sir Clive regarded Choo as dispensable too. She wondered if he knew Jake was the baby's father. Probably he did, and merely accepted it as a minor consideration. Leigh sighed. She appeared to be the only person perturbed by the situation. He used the Chinese girl purely for his own selfish ends, Leigh decided with a stab of anger. By continuing their relationship he had kept Choo under his influence because it suited him, but was prepared to cast her aside whenever he wished.

The following morning, when Leigh left the hospital, Bridget fussed around her as though she had just survived a major operation. Leigh accepted her administrations patiently, for her hostess was essentially a mother. She blossomed when there was someone to care for.

'Now you go and lie by the pool, my darlin',' she instructed, and Leigh was happy to do just that, though the whirl of thoughts which refused to desert her were unsettling. Wearily she decided she was becoming a little neurotic about Jake, and Choo, and the baby, and she tried hard to turn her mind to other topics, but it proved difficult. Despite a conspicuous absence of news about Jake, he was constantly in her thoughts. He could have sent a postcard, she thought irritably, to ask how I am. Time began to drag. Each passing hour was longer than the one before, and Leigh convinced herself that Jake had decided never to see her again. He would probably keep well away until she left Singapore. Uncomfortably she moved on the sunbed. She didn't want their relationship to end like that. How she wished she could rewrite her role in the past! She had seen the pain in Jake's eyes when she had accused him, a second time, of killing Patrick, and was filled with a desperate urge to tell him she had been wrong and ask his forgiveness. It was vital she leave the island with a clear conscience. Whatever Jake's faults, he didn't deserve to live with the misconception that she continued to blame him. She must apologise, although it was possible he would fling that apology right back in her face.

Perhaps he would contact her on Saturday, she thought hopefully, pulling at the towel with nervous fingers. He would be home with Benjy and could easily lift the telephone. Or should she telephone him? The whole of Friday was spent composing trite little apologies until Leigh lost patience with herself, and finally flung the whole stilted collection out of her mind in despair.

Saturday came and went. On several occasions she was tempted to lift the phone, but at the last moment her courage failed her. Jake's silence was indication enough that he considered their relationship over. Leigh sank into a lethargic, unsettled mood and was hard pressed to respond to Bridget's voluble chatter.

Sunday morning dawned, and her spirits divebombed as she glanced at the plane ticket on the dressing table. Her flight was scheduled for Tuesday, and now it was a cast-iron certainty she had seen the last of Jake, for he would be jetting off first thing Monday morning to some distant country on the next stage of his final tour.

It was with surprise she discovered Bridget busily amassing a picnic when she walked into the kitchen.

'We're all going out for the day,' her hostess sang, her bright curls bobbing as she scurried to and fro, fetching fresh fruit and bottles of drink.

'Where to?' Leigh sank down at the table, trying to adopt an air of interest. Her mood was so low she knew she would be bad company, she would be much better off spending the day huddled beneath the bedclothes.

'Panjang Island. Jake's taking us across in his speed-boat, surely you remember that he invited us a week or two ago.'

Leigh nodded, her heart knocking against her ribs as though trying to leap from her body. So she would see him again, and have a chance to apologise. 'Can I help make the sandwiches?' she asked, trying to control her sudden excitement. Her mind kicked over furiously as she buttered the bread. Then with a sickening clarity she realised that perhaps, yet again, Jake was merely carrying out his responsibilities, or, even worse, that Bridget had engineered the outing. 'Whose idea was this?' she asked casually, concentrating her attention on the wedge of beef pâté.

'Jake spoke to Frank,' Bridget told her. 'Benjy's been pestering him for us to all have a day out on the boat together.' She smiled at Leigh. 'It'll be good for you. It will cheer you up, stop you moping around.'

'I'm not moping,' Leigh muttered through clenched teeth.

Bridget sighed. 'You seem a touch melancholy to me, my darlin'. It's probably delayed reaction to your accident. You seem depressed.'

'I'm not,' Leigh snapped irritably, and was furious with herself when tears misted her eyes.

Jake was only taking them out because Benjy wanted it, the impetus had come from his son, not him. She squirmed in embarrassment, and wondered if she should plead a sudden, excruciating headache. Surely she could summon one up within minutes if she tried. No, that was impossible. Bridget would never believe her, and besides, it was better to set things straight, regardless of Jake's attitude. She would tell him how she felt, calmly and coolly, and that would be the end of that.

'Are you going to wear that itsy-bitsy bikini of yours?' Frank asked with a mock leer, sidling up and stealing a sandwich.

'For you, anything,' she smiled, dismissing her troubled thoughts.

'Hear that, Bridget? Eat your heart out!'

His wife chuckled. 'Then I shall put mine on, especially for Jake's benefit.'

Frank gave a snort of laughter. 'Heaven preserve us from forty-two-inch hips!' A hectic, cheerful fight followed and Leigh escaped to her room to change. She put her white satin bikini on beneath a navy blue vest and denim shorts, then slipped bare feet into a pair of flip-flop sandals and wriggled her toes. In England she was always layered in tights, skirt, sweater and invariably a jacket, but here in the heat she could be free. She found a sensual delight in the feel of the sun blazing down on bare arms and legs. A delight which would soon be terminated, she reminded herself, casting a wry glance at the plane ticket. She tied back her hair into a bouncing ponytail and pulled on a simple white peaked cap. Suntan lotion, dark glasses and towels were pushed into her canvas tote-bag, then she was ready.

'Where's her ladyship?' Frank demanded. He and

Leigh had been waiting patiently for fifteen minutes, but still Bridget didn't appear. 'No matter what time she starts getting ready, she's invariably late,' he complained.

'Don't mither!' Bridget appeared in the doorway of her room, an eye-catching figure in a full-length, electric blue kaftan and a frilly-brimmed straw hat. 'I'm ready now. Can you both give a hand with the coolbox and the bags?'

They reached the ground floor as Jake drew up in his gleaming Mercedes, with an excited Benjy bouncing up and down in the back seat.

'On time, for once,' Jake commented wryly, climbing out of the car as Bridget rushed to greet him, arms outstretched, pink-lipsticked mouth puckered in readiness. 'Quite a welcome,' he said, extricating himself from her embrace. His eyes flickered over Leigh. 'It's your turn now.' It was impossible to read his mood. He stood before her, tall and virile, the sun shining on his dark shining head. There was a challenge in his eyes. Once again he was forcing her to take a decision.

Leigh swallowed. With a swing of her hip she approached him boldly, slipping two arms around his neck and pulling his head down to hers. After all, she did love him, even if that love was doomed. She kissed him hard on the lips. For an instant Jake responded, then his long body stiffened and he calmly caught her arms and removed them from his neck. 'Don't get carried away,' he said sarcastically.

Leigh flushed scarlet. She could hardly blame Jake for his coolness, but there was no need for him to be cruel. Abruptly she turned from him, and went to help Frank stow the boxes in the car boot.

'Squeeze into the back with Benjy and me,' Bridget commanded, when the last box had been stacked away. 'Frank can go in the front.' Leigh clambered into the car where Benjy was jiggling up and down in excitement.

'We're going to Panjang Island,' he crowed. 'Then Daddy will take us out skiing from a tiny, tiny island near there. We've brought a big umbrella so you and Aunt Bridget can sit under it.' He twisted round to grin at her. 'And we've brought masses of beer and some wine, and Daddy says if we're all good he might take us out for dinner this evening.'

'Only might.' Jake turned the key in the ignition. 'Any misbehaviour from any of you,' he glanced round coolly to look straight into Leigh's eyes, 'and you'll go hungry.' The warning had been lightly given, but she was aware of a dangerous undercurrent in his words. Jake had taken control. It was apparent he would entertain no more of her fluctuating changes of heart. He would keep her at arm's length where he had kept her so successfully in the past.

'Are you fully recovered?' he asked politely, his eyes catching hers in the mirror.

'Yes, thank you.'

'Good.'

That was the sum total of his acknowledgement of her. Leigh sat quietly for the remainder of the drive to the coast. Everyone else chattered away, but she waited, hoping for some further comment from Jake, but he ignored her, entering into the general banter of conversation with such an air of enjoyment that she felt like thumping those wide shoulders and yelling 'What about me?' After a while she steeled herself to ignore him, too, and gazed out of the window, refusing to notice his competent hands on the wheel, the virile strength of his back.

Why have I fallen in love with him? she wondered despairingly, then supplied her own answer—because I can't help myself. The instant attraction she had felt when she first met him again in the lift had billowed so suddenly, so alarmingly, that it had overwhelmed her. Now she had no choice in the matter. She loved Jake with body and soul, that was all there was to it. And what a powerful, all-consuming emotion it was. The expression in his eyes when she had kissed him earlier had almost torn her apart, for she knew he had wanted her as desperately as she had wanted him. They were each totally involved with the other, and each knew it. There could be no half measures with a love like that; it had to be all or nothing. Leigh bit hard into her lip to keep away the tears. Nothing, she thought miserably, that was what the future must hold—nothing.

It had been so different when she had fallen in love with Patrick. They had known each other from schooldays and had started going out together in a crowd, pairing off almost by chance. Gradually their friendship had ripened into love. Patrick seemed to have always been a part of her life, warm and friendly, and marrying him was an extension of that feeling. Their relationship had followed predictable lines, and she didn't doubt that, had he lived, they would have grown old together—friends as well as lovers.

But in retrospect she wondered if that secure, companionable love would have continued to satisfy her completely. Jake had roused emotions she had scarcely known she possessed, making her aware of the true strength of love, both spiritual and physical. She had never felt more sure of herself as a woman, a passionate, uninhibited woman, than when they had given each other the gift of love in Hong Kong.

Leigh rested her burning forehead on the cool glass of the car window. Loving Jake was like being consumed by a tropical fever where one had lucid crystal clear moments, followed by ravaging excesses of imagination. Sensibly she knew she must reject their love and leave him to deal with Choo and the baby in his own way. Doubtless in time she would meet someone else, someone without moral ties. Leigh closed her eyes. What was the point of deceiving herself? If Jake was denied her, then she knew no other man could ever be anything but second best. Casting a resentful glance at the back of his dark head she admitted Jake was a far more virile character than Patrick had ever been. It wasn't merely a question of his successful career. Jake's personality was more definite, more forceful, and this had awakened a corresponding need in her. Sir Clive had said Jake required a partner, someone with spirit, and

Leigh knew deep down that they were well matched. Her throat was paralysed with pain. If only everything was straightforward! If only Choo had never happened. If only, if only. For a long time she turned the situation over and over in her mind, but there was no way out.

On their arrival at the boatyard Jake parked in the shade of a palm tree, and organised the speedboat. Then everyone helped carry the bags and boxes to the water's edge. When the boat was launched they removed their sandals and waded through the warm shallow water to climb aboard.

'We should manage to fit in. Although it would have been easier if Bridget had kept to that diet of hers.' Jake raised a brow, making the butt of his joke wrinkle her nose goodnaturedly at him. 'Hold on to your hats, folks!' He started the engine.

'That means you, Aunt Bridget,' Benjy whispered, glancing up at the large straw hat. The boat surged forward. Panjang Island was ten minutes' sail from the mainland. It was a long thin spit of land with a natural rocky bay at one end, and had been developed by the government to provide a holiday resort for day trippers. There were man-made swimming lagoons on each side of the central ridge, and a collection of wooden beach huts and food stalls. Lacy casuarina trees grew along the shores, providing shelter from the hot sun. When Jake cut the engine Benjy was first out of the boat.

'The sand's burning!' he squealed, leaping up and down.

'Wear your sandals,' his father said sternly. Benjy slipped them on, then grabbed Leigh's hand and began pulling her up the beach.

'Let's go and climb the rocks,' he pleaded.

'Put your tee-shirt on first,' Jake commanded. 'Keep it on all the time, even in the water—remember you burnt your back when we were here before.'

Reluctantly the little boy released her hand and waited impatiently for Jake to join them. He hopped about, first on one foot, and then the other, while Jake struggled to fit his arms into the holes.

'Here, let me.' Leigh bent forward and deftly fitted the shirt over Benjy's thin chest.

'That's right,' he smiled up at her. 'Daddy's hands are too big.'

'Nothing like a woman's touch,' Bridget remarked airily as she passed by carrying a picnic hamper, and Jake's face darkened with hidden anger.

'The rocks, the rocks!' chanted Benjy.

'Be quiet!' His father's curt tone silenced him.

'I'll come later,' Leigh promised, keeping a watchful eye on Jake as he went back down to the boat to help Frank unload the gear. A nerve that flickered in his jaw indicated he was in no mood to be treated carelessly. He would dictate the action, or not play at all.

In a few minutes the umbrella was in place, and the coolboxes and hampers carefully stashed in the shade. Leigh spread wide towels on the sand and lay down.

'Paradise!' Bridget sighed, sitting beside her. 'Look at the colours in that sea—everything from deep blue to pale turquoise.' Even Frank raised his head from a book to admire the brilliant colours.

'Can I go first on the skis, Daddy? Please, can I? Please?' Benjy demanded eagerly, jumping up and down.

'Okay.' Jake was calm again, the flash of anger had subsided. He pulled off his tee-shirt, revealing a deeply tanned body. Leigh watched him secretly through her lashes, remembering the feel of his hairy chest. 'Do you mind coming along too, Frank?' Jake asked. 'As a precautionary measure. Benjy tends to get carried away at times.'

'Sure, no problem.' Frank heaved himself off the sand and stripped down to his trunks, then he made a playful grab for the little boy and swung him in the air. Benjy squealed excitedly. The three of them clambered into the boat, and it roared away, churning up a plume of white spray. Benjy's shrill voice pierced the drone of the engine for a few seconds, then faded into the distance.

'Fancy a walk, my darlin'?' Bridget asked.

'Not really,' Leigh replied.

'Good, neither do I. I want to get on with my needle-point.' She pulled a polythene bag from one of the boxes and took out her canvas and wools. As Bridget started to thread her needle Leigh lay back again on the towel, luxuriating in the warmth of the sun. The island was almost deserted. The only other group on the beach was a party of Malay women, sitting beneath parasols in the distance. She felt drowsy and closed her eyes, lulled by the gentle lapping of the waves on the shore. She must have dozed, for in no time at all she heard the thrum of the engine, and dragged herself awake. Idly she sat up, leaning back on her elbows, watching the sea and the progress of the boat through the waves. As soon as it stopped Benjy jumped out into the water and charged through the shallows like a mad thing.

'I stayed up for one whole minute!' he yelled excitedly. Frank, who was close behind, caught most of his splashing, but he was laughing too, enjoying the fun.

'We all had a go, even Uncle Frank.' Benjy ran up the beach and threw himself down on the towel beside Leigh. 'I was good, wasn't I, Daddy?' he shouted.

'You did very well,' Jake agreed from the shallows, where he was holding the boat. 'Come on, Bridget, it's your turn now.' Almost as an afterthought he added, 'And you, too, Leigh.'

'Will you take me to the rocks while they're gone, Uncle Frank?' Benjy asked, scrambling to his feet. 'Then we can climb.'

'All right, but you'll have to show me the way.' Frank held out his hand and the little boy grabbed it, and with backward smiles the two of them disappeared into the trees.

'Come on!' Jake shouted impatiently. Leigh stood up and slowly pulled off her vest and shorts. The bikini beneath was tiny, with a halter neck. Small gold buckles secured the triangles clinging to her hips. She licked her lips nervously, conscious of Jake's eyes upon her. He seemed to be hypnotised, then he dragged his gaze away and shouted again, 'Hurry up, Bridget!'

'I'll not bother today, Jake darlin', if you don't mind. My back's been playing up again. You take Leigh.'

'Okay.' He sounded bad-tempered.

Leigh pulled the band from her ponytail and the hair fell heavily, swirling around her shoulders in auburn waves. She walked down the beach towards him, head held erect. He'd damn well have to notice her now, she thought rebelliously. He was silent, but as he put out a hand to help her climb aboard she recognised desire in his glittering gaze. Jake stared at her, then his eyes narrowed with suspicion.

'What the hell do you think you're playing at now?' he snarled, glancing towards the beach to make sure they were out of earshot. Bridget was engrossed, head down, in her needlepoint. Leigh was hotly aware of Jake's eyes touring her body.

'I'm wearing a swimsuit, because I intend to go swimming,' she replied coldly. The air was charged with static. She was sure if she touched him she'd get an electric shock.

'You're deliberately trying to arouse me.' The words were a growl that started deep in his chest.

'I am not!'

'Oh no?' The look in his eyes made her turn away. 'Two can play at that game,' he snapped, 'and as you appear to prefer sex without any other commitment you can't blame me if I enter wholeheartedly into the fun.'

Savagely he thrust the speedboat into gear, and they shot away, skimming across the water. Leigh clung to the safety bar in front of her, arms tense, knuckles white. The wind whipped out her hair into a pale golden banner.

'Ever made love on the ocean?' Jake asked drily, his gaze stripping the bikini from her until she felt naked and frighteningly vulnerable. It had been a mistake to wear it, she should have been more prudent. By now Jake had probably decided she was loose. She bit deeply into her lip as she said the word to herself. After all, she had admitted she wanted him, she had slept with him, but she refused to marry him. He couldn't be blamed for reaching the wrong conclusion.

'Like to try now?' Jake lifted his foot from the pedal and the boat slowed, sinking to rest in the water. There was something she didn't like in his tone, an underlying harshness that scared her.

'No,' she replied in a weak voice, avoiding the gray eyes which continued to rove her curves. She looked around in consternation. The nearest land was a blur on the horizon. There were no other boats in sight. Jake stretched out an arm, pulling her against the hardness of his chest. His hands urgently caressed the naked flesh of her arms, her shoulders, her back.

'Damn you,' he muttered angrily, 'you're like a drug. I can't get you out of my system, though heaven knows I want to.' He lowered his mouth to hers, forcing her lips open in a bruising rapacity that contained not one iota of tenderness.

'No, Jake, I don't want to,' she pleaded, pushing him away.

'You always say no at the beginning,' he sneered. 'But I'm sure I can persuade you to change your mind, you're very good at that.' He pulled her close again. His mouth was hot against her cheek, and then he lowered his head and bit her bare shoulder. She winced at the pain and forced him away.

'I'm an ardent lover,' he taunted, 'you know that. You mustn't blame me if I get carried away.'

'Can't we talk?' she implored. His restless anger was sending daggers of fear along her backbone.

'Talk! Who the hell needs to talk?'

'I do.'

He lifted a sardonic brow. 'You've said enough, Leigh. I know you'll take me as your lover, but never as your husband, so let's just forget it all, shall we? I should have had the sense to realise our relationship was doomed from the start.' He shrugged. 'The sex is very good, but that's about as far as it goes.' The innate cruelty of his words made her grow cold inside.

'I want to apologise,' she said in a low voice. 'I behaved stupidly when I accused you of involvement in

Patrick's death. I've thought it all out, and I know I was wrong.'

'How very decent of you!' He curled his lip. 'So I'm to be given absolution, am I? Your generosity is overwhelming. After two years I'm to be forgiven for a crime I never committed in the first place.'

'I stopped blaming you a long time ago,' she justified.

'Indeed?' His eyes were like ice floes. 'You have a strange way of showing it.'

'I'm sorry.'

'So you should be.' He leaned forward and gunned the engine, making the boat throb to life. Tears of frustration welled in Leigh's eyes, but they were immediately swept away by the whiplash of the wind. She glanced fearfully at Jake, wondering if she dared continue the conversation, but the angry expression on his face stopped her.

The boat surged across the waves. How could she tell him that her objection to marrying him had nothing to do with Patrick, but everything to do with Choo? He looked so furious that she knew if she started to explain that dilemma he'd probably dump her overboard immediately. Perhaps she could write it all down in a letter and post it to him when she was back home? She gave a shaky sigh.

'Have you water-skied before?' he shouted at last, over the roar of the engine.

'Yes.'

'In that case don't bother with a lifejacket, it cuts down your mobility.' His eyes swept scornfully over the minuscule bikini. 'I don't imagine that wisp you're wearing will get in the way.'

He dismissed her again, turning away to concentrate on the boat. Leigh raised her face to the sun. It felt good, and despite the perplexity of her emotions, the speed of the boat, the wind in her hair, the scattered flick of the surf on her face began to revive her spirits. Her lips moved into a spontaneous smile.

Jake noticed her pleasure. 'I shall miss all this when I return to England,' he said ruefully, the wide sweep of his arm encompassing the white-topped waves, the deep blue sky, the distant islands with their fringe of golden sand and topknots of swaying palms.

'I'm sure you will,' she agreed, 'but it's a marvellous promotion, you must be very pleased.'

'I am,' he admitted cryptically, but she was relieved to notice his harsh anger was beginning to seep away.

When they reached the small island he secured the boat, and they jumped out into the shallows. He helped Leigh fit on the skis.

'It's a long time since I've done this,' she said. 'You'll have to refresh my memory.'

He stood close behind her, his arms parallel with hers. 'Relax, bend a little at the knees. Keep your arms straight, and take a firm grip.' For a moment Leigh thought she felt the brush of his lips in her hair, but when she turned her head he moved away and returned to the boat.

'Hold on tight!' he shouted as she felt the drag of the rope through the water. The first attempt was disastrous. Her legs had a will of their own, and moved stubbornly in opposite directions. She was forced to let go of the bar and sank giggling into the waves.

'Everything okay?' Jake circled the boat back to her. 'Try again.'

'I feel such an idiot,' she shouted, 'two seconds up, then splash!'

'Don't worry. There's only me here, and I certainly don't care.' He grinned at her from the boat. 'It took me ages before I got the hang of it. For some reason I persisted in lifting one leg. I looked like an overgrown ostrich zooming around!'

Leigh laughed and tried again. Jake was endlessly patient. She had three or four tries, and her confidence grew. On the fifth occasion she managed to remain upright for several minutes before he switched off the engine and she slid slowly back into the sea.

'Clever girl!' he shouted, bringing the boat close. He looked down at her, doggy-paddling in the deep blue water, and his mouth twisted with amusement at one corner. She smiled back.

'Shall I get in?'

He made no move to assist, but sat grinning down.

'Help me, then.' She lifted her arms up towards him. Jake's eyes darkened, making her suddenly wary.

'I suggested you make yourself decent—well, half decent at least, before joining me, otherwise I might not be responsible for my actions. I'm only flesh and blood, after all.' His eyes slid down her body, feasting on the twin globes of her breasts. With horror she realised the halter strap of her bikini had come adrift and the top was floating around her ribcage. Leigh fumbled in the water for the straps.

'Can I help?' he asked nonchalantly, leaning back and enjoying her confusion. She flushed, feeling a stab of anger at his smug delight. Twisting furiously in the water, she turned her tanned back on him, pulling the top back into position.

'All safely tucked in, or would you like me to put everything back in its proper place?' he grinned.

'Damn you!' she snapped, annoyed with her embarrassment as he pulled her up into the boat beside him.

'Why damn me?' he asked innocently, the quirk of laughter still playing on his lips. 'It's not my fault if you choose to charge around clad only in four minuscule scraps of material, and then to reveal those tantalising breasts.' He put out a finger and slipped it insolently beneath the thin white satin, teasing her nipple until it hardened.

Leigh pushed his hand away angrily. 'I didn't choose to reveal anything,' she retorted, stung by the easy familiarity of his gesture.

He shrugged. 'Even when the bikini is in position you don't leave much to the imagination, do you?' he mocked. Abruptly the amusement dropped from his voice and his face became pensive. He put a hand on either side of her head and drew her towards him. She could feel his heart pounding erratically within his chest, joining the jungle rhythm that filled her ears. 'I want you, my beautiful girl,' he said fiercely. 'I want you so much.' His hands were trembling.

Leigh tried to snatch at the last remnants of coherent thought which were rapidly being diminished by his demanding mouth. She clung to him, unable to resist, her body fiery with his kisses and the blaze of the tropical sun overhead.

'It's no use,' Jake groaned at length, dragging himself away from her. 'There's no way we can make love in a rocking boat, but tonight we'll get rid of Bridget and Frank, and you'll come home with me. We'll put Benjy in bed and barricade his door.' He gave a grin. 'Then we can be alone. Choo's staying out overnight.'

Choo! Leigh stared at him in dismay. So while Choo was conveniently out of Jake's house she would be in it, making love. Never!

'I can't,' she said firmly, tightening her lips.

'Don't be prudish,' he teased. 'Relax, my love. We're two grown up people, Leigh, we're not breaking any laws by loving each other. We've cleared that business about Patrick's death out of the way, and now there's nothing to stop us getting married—and we will be, soon, I promise you.'

Leigh took a deep breath. 'I can't marry you, Jake.'

His mood changed like a dark cloud covering the sun. He clenched his teeth and glared at her. 'That's it!' he growled. 'I shan't ask you again.'

'Please, Jake, let me explain,' she begged.

'Explain!' The word sounded like an oath. 'Don't waste your breath. I don't need an explanation. Either you love me and want to marry me, or you don't. I'm not interested in anything else.'

With a furious movement he gunned the engine into life before Leigh had time to protest.

'I'm sorry,' she said eventually.

'And so you bloody well should be!' he retorted angrily. Leigh's temper rose and she flashed him a glance of attack. True, she was sorry, but she wasn't prepared to grovel. She wanted to explain, but not when he was in this mood, darkly sullen, his fury standing between them like a solid wall of steel.

'When you've calmed down I'll. . . .' Her voice petered out beneath the violence of his glare.

'You'll what?' he demanded roughly. 'You'll make love to me one moment and reject me the next? To hell with that for a game! It's obvious peaceful co-existence is impossible between us, and, quite frankly, I don't give a damn.'

Leigh started to speak, but he rounded on her.

'Shut up!' he ordered, in a voice so savage that she was left breathless.

Neither of them looked at each other again on the journey back to Panjang Island. Each was involved in his own thoughts. Jake's hurt and furious exasperation were written all over him. Leigh lowered her head in shame. She hadn't meant to cause him pain, but there was no alternative, even if she had managed to explain her feelings about Choo she knew he would still have been angry. How could you tell a man you loved him, but not enough to ignore his treatment of his mistress? It didn't make sense to her, so she was sure it wouldn't to him.

When they were a fair distance from the shore he silenced the engine. 'Let's keep it cool,' he snapped as the boat drifted inwards. 'There's no point spoiling everyone's day.'

'Fine.' Leigh forced a weak smile which Jake patently ignored. She jumped over the side of the boat and swam rapidly towards the shore, leaving him frowning after her.

She was surprised at her acting ability, and Jake's too, for that matter, for they both managed to get through the rest of the day with apparent ease. Even Bridget appeared to detect nothing unusual in their behaviour towards each other. Leigh had deliberately blotted out her feelings, and after a few tentative comments managed to speak and joke with Jake with an amazing degree of normality. He was his usual mocking self, making jokes that had Benjy giggling ecstatically, and indulging in wry comments at Bridget's expense.

'You and I live on a different plane, Bridget,' he

drawled, as they sat around drinking a final beer in the late afternoon. The older woman had blithely taken yet another dose of his outrageous teasing as the literal truth. Bridget was not at all perturbed, and merely put out an elbow to dig him firmly in the ribs. Jake rolled away, as if in pain, moaning loudly, and Benjy clambered forward to sit firmly astride his chest as he lay spreadeagled on the sand.

'Which plane are you on, Daddy?' he asked, puzzled, 'a jumbo jet?'

Everyone laughed.

'We're all on different planes,' Jake answered, grinning up at his son. 'You and I are British Airways. Aunt Bridget is Aer Lingus because she has a touch of the blarney. Uncle Frank is Singapore Airlines, because he fancies all the girls in their sarongs, and Leigh . . .' He paused, glancing across at her from beneath his lashes. 'I guess she must be one of the American airlines, smart and sassy as hell—fly me, I'm Leigh.' He raised a scornful brow, and she stuck out her tongue at him. The provocation in his voice made her want to fling herself upon him and hammer at his chest with protesting fists.

'It's time to pack up now, it'll soon be dark,' Jake said crisply, as though reading her thoughts. He lifted Benjy from his chest and set him down on the sand.

'Can I have one last swim? Please, please!' begged Benjy.

'A quick one,' Jake agreed, 'while we load the boat.'

'Swim with me, Leigh,' Benjy commanded, putting out his hand to pull her up. She rose reluctantly.

'I must help with the gear.'

'Go with him, I don't like him to be alone in deep water,' Jake commanded tartly. You mean you don't want me near you, Leigh thought belligerently. She flushed. There was no reason for him to be so objectionable.

'Beat you into the sea!' she challenged Benjy, and together they ran down the beach and into the water.

CHAPTER NINE

'I'M the winner!' Benjy crowed as he scampered through the shallows. The sandy ocean floor dropped away abruptly and Leigh dived forward into deep water. When she emerged he was beside her, swimming with quick movements of thin arms and legs.

She tucked her wet hair smoothly behind her ears. 'This is far enough,' she warned, for they were well out of their depth.

'I'm a good swimmer,' he assured her.

'I know, but we shouldn't go too far out, in case there's a current. Let's turn round and I'll race you back to shore.'

With lightning speed Benjy twisted and began swimming towards the beach. Leigh did a careful breaststroke, deliberately keeping a short distance behind him. It would do no harm to let him imagine he had beaten her. He glanced over his shoulder, his face alive with delight, but when he was two or three yards ahead his small body suddenly jack-knifed and his head disappeared beneath the water. Leigh's heart contracted with fear, and she swam towards him with quick strong strokes. It flashed through her mind that he must be having a convulsion. Jake had been wrong, both his sons had inherited the same weakness. As she reached the struggling child she tried to hold him, but panic had made him strong and he twisted and turned viciously, gasping for breath. At last she managed to pull him against her chest, as she paddled frantically with her feet to keep them both afloat.

'My leg, my leg!' Benjy spluttered.

'What's wrong?' Leigh demanded, trying to swim towards shallower water in vain as his arms and legs continued to beat against her, threatening to break her grasp. She thrust a hand beneath his body, and saw that one of his legs was slashed with a deep pink whiplash.

'It hurts,' he whimpered. His thin arms came around her neck, clinging on desperately, forcing her head beneath the waves. Now it was her turn to struggle. She kicked with her legs and rose to the surface, choking on salt water. Again she felt herself sinking, the small arms tightly gripping her neck, cutting off the air supply. Leigh was terrified, then strong hands slid beneath her armpits, and she was lifted bodily until her head was clear of the water. She coughed and spluttered, catching her breath. Jake was beside her. He held her close for a moment or two until she recovered, then took Benjy from her arms.

'It was a jellyfish,' Leigh babbled, 'on his leg.'

Jake raised his son in the water. 'Nothing serious,' he said, though his expression was strained. 'It's not poisonous, the pain will soon wear off. He'll be fine in a moment, won't you, Benjy?'

Benjy raised his head from Jake's shoulder and gave a thin smile.

Leigh closed her eyes in relief.

'Are you all right?' Jake asked worriedly, touching her shoulder.

She nodded weakly. 'I'm okay, let's get back to shore.'

Jake swam protectively beside her, the whimpering Benjy clinging on to his back.

Bridget and Frank were waiting on the beach, watching their progress.

'What's happened?' Bridget demanded. 'We heard Benjy crying. Come to Aunt Bridget, my love.' She held out her arms, but the little boy clung tightly to Jake's shoulders.

'A jellyfish caught his leg,' Jake explained. 'I suspect it was more shock than injury.' He looked down at the damp head on his chest. 'I dare say after a good night's sleep he'll be back to his usual livewire self.'

Benjy gave a flicker of a smile.

'Home,' Bridget decided. 'The sooner he's tucked up in bed, the better.'

'Stand down, Benjy,' Jake said gently. 'I must drive the boat.'

'I want Leigh to carry me.' Benjy stuck out his lower lip and raised his arms. When she took him he buried his face in her shoulder, his arms fastening like a vice around her neck.

'You don't mind having him?' Jake pushed his hand through his hair in a quick gesture. 'He's not too heavy?' Leigh shook her head silently, and Jake produced a weak smile of gratitude.

Frank placed the final picnic box into the boat and clambered aboard as Jake started the engine. Leigh sat in the back seat beside Bridget, Benjy clinging to her. When she bent her head and softly kissed his hair he gave a little smile.

'Do you feel better now?' she asked. He nodded and sank back, snuggling against her warm wet body.

The return journey was accomplished without further mishap, and Bridget and Leigh waited on the shore as the two men unloaded the boat and hauled it back into the boathouse. Despite Bridget's repeated persuasions Benjy refused to leave Leigh's arms.

'I must put some clothes on,' she told him gently. 'I can't go back to town in my bikini. Go to Aunt Bridget for a moment.'

Bridget held out her arms.

'No,' Benjy muttered, burrowing his head in Leigh's shoulder.

Jake paused in packing the boat and came over. 'Don't be silly,' he said, firmly lifting the small wriggling frame from her. Quickly Leigh rifled through her tote-bag for shorts and vest, putting them on over the almost dry bikini. Her sea-soaked hair had dried in the sun and badly needed attention, but there was no time for vanity now, and she quickly twisted it into a long plait and flicked it back over her shoulder. Benjy watched intently as she slipped on her flip-flops, then he launched himself from Jake's arms into hers.

'Can I have a towel, Jake?' she asked. 'Benjy's clothes are damp, he might feel cold if he's not wrapped up.'

Jake provided a large beach towel from the boot of the car.

'Sit in front,' Bridget instructed. 'There's more room.'

Leigh sat down in the front passenger seat, with Benjy wrapped up on her knee, and Frank and Bridget settled themselves in behind. As Jake started the car darkness was falling and the street lights were flickering on.

'I'm afraid we'll have to cancel that dinner date,' Jake commented as they reached the suburbs. 'Benjy's in no fit state for socialising.' He gave a quick glance at his son, who was fast asleep on Leigh's lap, his little face tranquil, his thumb in his mouth.

'No, no, it's out of the question,' Frank quickly agreed. 'Best idea is for you to drop Bridget and me off at home, and then take Leigh back to your place. It's a shame to disturb Benjy now.' He leaned forward. 'Is that okay with you, Leigh? You can help Jake get that young man to bed, and then I'll come for you later.'

'That would be great,' Jake put in quickly. 'I'm sorry I'm not able to deliver Leigh back myself, but Sunday is Choo's night off, and I can't leave Benjy alone in the house.'

Leigh acquiesced with a smile. It would have been churlish to refuse to fall in with the plan.

Jake dropped the O'Briens off at their apartment with a minimum of fuss, then pulled the car quickly back on to the road. He put out a hand and touched Benjy's warm cheek. 'I can't bear it when anything happens to him,' he said tersely, looking straight ahead. 'When he hurts himself, even a little, it really chews me up.'

'Don't worry,' Leigh said gently. 'He'll be all right.' She loosened the towel. 'See, the mark's fading already.'

'I know,' said Jake on a note of despair, 'but if I lost him I'd have no one.'

'You'd have Choo,' she retorted, 'and the baby.'

Jake gave her a long hard look but said nothing. When they arrived at the house he parked at the front door and came round to her. 'Shall I take him?'

Benjy was disturbed by the sudden lack of motion and opened two blue eyes. 'I want Leigh,' he demanded.

'I'll carry him,' she told Jake, and followed him into the house. He switched on some lights, then shepherded

her up the stairs to Benjy's bedroom. The little boy had
fallen asleep again.

'We'd better undress him,' she whispered, laying him
on the bed, 'his clothes are still damp.' Benjy stirred as
she gently removed his beach clothes. Jake produced
clean pyjamas and helped her put them on him. She
pulled up the sheet, smiling down at the soft little face,
while Jake stood silently by, watching her, his mouth
straight and noncommittal. Leigh knelt down to kiss
the smooth cheek and Benjy smiled in his sleep. Jake
put his arm around her shoulder as they walked back
down the stairs to the lounge.

'Thank you,' he said huskily. 'I honestly don't know
what I would have done without you.'

'Benjy's a lovely little boy.' She turned to him, speaking crisply. 'I'll go now. Can I telephone Frank and ask
him to collect me?'

'Don't leave yet,' said Jake, avoiding her eyes. 'Can I
get you something to eat?'

She shook her head. They were both weary, drained
by the day in the sun and the upheaval with Benjy. She
was vulnerable—too vulnerable, for already Jake's
nearness was reducing her to a quivering wreck.

'How about a drink?' he persisted, taking hold of her
hand. 'You're going home on Tuesday, surely we can
part as friends?' His thumb caressed the palm, sending
shivers of longing through her. 'Stay with me for a while,
please. I promise I won't touch you, if that's what you're
afraid of.' He raised both hands above his head and
stepped back, his mouth curving into a smile. 'See, I'll
be a good boy.'

Leigh gave a tremulous grin. 'How can I resist? I'll
have a brandy, please. And while you're pouring it I'll
go and tidy up, I feel like a wreck.'

'You look beautiful,' he assured her.

Her hair was sticky with salt, but she combed it
several times and left it loose around her shoulders. All
vestige of the mascara and lip-gloss which she had
applied that morning had disappeared, and after a good
wash her face was scrubbed and shining. Two goblets of

brandy were waiting on the long low table when she returned, and she sat down opposite Jake, her golden legs stretched out tiredly before her.

'What a day!' Jake rubbed the back of his neck as the atmosphere stretched tautly between them. Leigh took a gulp of brandy. 'Did you know it was a jellyfish that had hurt him, when Benjy started to thrash around?' he asked.

She shook her head. 'I thought he was having a convulsion,' she said in a low voice, 'like Choo's baby. Your other son.'

Jake's head jerked up and he stared at her. 'My *other* son?' he said incredulously, then his face tightened. 'Is that what you think? That Choo and I are lovers?' Leigh nodded weakly.

'This is one of my darlin' Bridget's theories, isn't it?' he demanded, glowering at her with furious expression. 'My darling, Leigh, I said once you had some incredible blind spots, but this beats the lot, you bloody specialise in them!'

'But Choo lives here,' she protested, 'and you pay for the baby's hospital treatment.'

With one quick movement he moved across and sat beside her, his eyes burning with anger. 'Don't you think you ought to check up on Bridget's wild ideas?'

'How can I?' The reply was hot, fuelled by his annoyance.

'You could have asked me.'

'And what would I have said?' she enquired, lifting her chin defensively. 'Please, Mr St John, is Choo your mistress?'

He sighed and gave a thin smile. 'Perhaps it's not after-dinner conversation, but for heaven's sake, Leigh, we know each other well enough to be frank.'

'Not that frank!' she retorted.

He stretched out a hand, and traced a slow path down her cheekbone. 'Rory is the father of Choo's baby.'

'Rory!' She gazed at him in amazement.

'Yes,' he said heavily, 'though when her pregnancy was first discovered he strongly denied any responsibility. However, Choo comes from a good family and Rory was her only boy-friend, so his denial was complete poppycock. I've known her father for several years and when Rory refused to have anything to do with the expected child I felt the company should try and help. I had a discreet word with Sir Clive, and he agreed that Milwain International would foot the bill for her confinement.'

'Sir Clive knows?' Leigh's grey eyes were startled.

Jake shrugged. 'I gathered Rory had been in trouble once before, so it wasn't a complete surprise. To cut a long story short, when the child was born Rory admitted it was his and began to show a renewed interest in Choo.'

'She is a pretty little thing,' she agreed.

Jake pulled a wry face. 'That's the problem. I was worried then that she might have a second love-child by him, so I ordered him to keep well away from her.'

'But he didn't?'

'No,' he admitted with a grimace. 'With regard to the hospital bills, I do pay them, but Rory reimburses me. Sir Clive wanted it that way, to try and avoid any scandal. Obviously he'd forgotten about Bridget's overactive imagination!'

'What will happen to Choo when you return to England?' Leigh asked.

'She's going to Bali.'

'With Rory!'

'Yes.' Jake twisted his mouth. 'It appears she's still hooked on him and apparently is content to hang around until he decides whether or not he wants to marry her.' His long fingers urgently caressed the smooth skin at the nape of her neck. 'I know just how she feels,' he continued, bending his dark head and kissing her forehead. 'I'm just as hooked up on you, my beautiful girl. If you won't marry me, at least live with me,' he said desperately. 'It goes against the grain, I admit, I'm a conventional kind of guy at heart, but I don't think I can live without you.'

His mouth sought hers, and his kiss convinced her for

ever that he loved her, that he would take her on whatever terms she wished. When eventually he released her Leigh smiled, her eyes sparkling.

'Do you really mean that as Chairman of Milwain International you'd have me as your mistress?' she teased.

'I don't care about Milwain International,' Jake muttered, his mouth moving over hers. 'All I care about is you.'

'I'll marry you, my darling,' Leigh whispered, her arms twined around his neck. 'I only refused because of Choo, I thought your place was with her.'

'No, it's with you,' he said happily, holding her close. 'I've known that for the past two years. And even before,' he admitted. 'I fancied you when you were here with Patrick.'

Leigh's eyes opened wide in surprise.

'Surely you noticed all the girl-friends?' he asked drily. 'I embarked on a great sexual binge to wear out my desire, but when I closed my eyes I found myself pretending it was you, which didn't help at all.' He grimaced. 'I was frightened of touching you, even accidentally, in case in some way I transmitted my feelings. I needn't have bothered. You were far too wrapped up in Patrick, thank goodness. I certainly had no wish to come between you.'

Leigh looked at him for a long moment. 'Supposing I'd met someone back in England?'

'I would have flown over on the first plane.' Jake's voice was firm. 'Why do you imagine I showed such interest in your letters to Bridget? I was keeping track of you.'

'But why didn't you visit me and explain how you felt?' Leigh put her head on one side and studied him.

The corner of Jake's mouth moved in a dismissive gesture. 'I reckoned that at first you were too distraught to consider a second romance and then, as time passed, I began to feel apprehensive about approaching you. I didn't want to travel all the way to England and have you slam the door in my face. It seemed one hell of a gamble.' He gave a sheepish grin. 'So I persuaded Bridget to invite you over here. I thought I stood a better chance of sweeping you off your feet when you were on holiday.'

'You engineered my visit!'

'Not completely.' Jake gave an embarrassed shrug. 'I hinted that a month in the sun might do you good, and gradually Bridget came to believe it was her idea in the first place.'

'You really are worse than she is—talk about manipulation!' Leigh laughed delightedly.

'I had it all planned. I was going to play it very cool and controlled.' He lifted a self-mocking brow. 'But I ended up making love to you, and then yelling at you.'

'I didn't help much, did I?'

'You certainly didn't!' Jake retorted with feeling. 'I never knew where I was with you. Well, that's not quite true. It was blatantly obvious the physical attraction was strong, but the circumstances, and Bridget's meddling, kept getting in the way.'

Leigh pursed her lips. 'What about Rory—you didn't arrange some competition for yourself, too, did you?'

Jake laughed, his eyes gleaming. 'Hell, no! I'd forgotten about Bridget's love of matchmaking, and when, in her wisdom, she decided you and Rory might click my plans were suddenly in danger. I was terrified you might fall for him. That's why I tried to convince you he was a lightweight, not worthy of consideration.'

'Did you send him off to Taiwan on purpose?' Leigh asked, her mouth moving with amusement.

He hesitated, his confusion transparent as he considered his reply. Finally he shook his head in exasperation. 'Well, yes.' He changed his mind. 'No. Oh hell, partly.' He glanced at her. 'His visit wasn't vital, I just wanted him out of the way. I was jealous as hell, so I came on as the big boss and wielded the stick. I'm sure Rory knew, but he was in no position to argue.'

Jake looked so shamefaced that she started to laugh.

'On the face of it, Rory is quite a catch,' he justified, then his eyes crinkled at the corners as he joined in her amusement.

'But I didn't want to catch anyone.'

'You made that abundantly clear the first time we met,' Jake said drily. 'You were scared to death of being hurt again. I knew how you felt, I'd been there myself. There was a time in my life when I swore I'd never fall in love again. It was too painful. But as time went by I began to understand that there are no half measures, either you care for someone so much it hurts, or you don't. You can't escape it.' He pushed his fingers into her hair and pulled her close. 'I love you.'

'I didn't want to fall in love with you, Jake,' Leigh murmured, tracing the outline of his lips with her index finger.

'I know. I was so furious when you returned and still felt bitter towards me, I wanted to rant and rave at you for being so unfair. I guess we all tend to lash out blindly when we're hurt, you lashed out at me, that's all.'

His hands slid beneath her vest and released the catch of her bikini top, then his fingers began to move insistently across her breasts. His kisses covered her fiery body until she cried out with soft moans of desire.

'I want you,' Leigh whispered as he relentlessly carried her onward to a place where there was only the two of them, kissing, touching, moving together. His hands were on her hips when the telephone rang.

'Not now,' he groaned, his fingers silkily stroking her burning flesh until Leigh felt she was drowning in him, her senses reeling beneath the determined attack of his mouth, his hands. The telephone rang and rang.

'Leave it,' she begged, as he paused and the urgency of his hands faltered.

'It'll be Frank. If I don't answer Benjy might wake up.'

'Leave it, darling.' Leigh moved her fingers over him, arousing him deliberately, feeling the hard muscles throb with excitement, but the telephone never stopped.

Jake lifted his head from her. 'I must answer it.' He moved away and dimly Leigh heard him lift the receiver. 'Hello, Frank,' he said in a remarkably normal voice. 'Okay, that's fine. See you.' Leigh lifted her arms around his neck as he returned to sit beside her, his dark eyes intense with longing.

'Oh Leigh, I want to make love to you,' he groaned, as his lips returned to hers, 'but we can't, not tonight.'

'Why?'

Reluctantly he pulled away. 'Frank's coming to collect you in twenty minutes.'

Leigh moaned in frustration.

'Believe me, it's better this way, my darling,' Jake said huskily. 'I'm desperate to make love to you, but not like this, not here. Benjy might wake up, and in any case I'm too long in the tooth to derive much satisfaction from a quick skirmish.' He lifted his brows ruefully. 'I want you all to myself, for hours on end.'

'I suppose you're right,' Leigh admitted shakily.

'I am,' he said, kissing the corner of her mouth. 'You'd better make yourself respectable before Frank appears.' He fastened the catch at the nape of her neck. 'We'll be married as soon as is humanly possible,' he assured her, holding her tight.

'But I'm going home on Tuesday,' she complained, as the sudden realisation of their parting hit her.

'Cancel it.'

'I can't,' she moaned. 'My boss will be returning from the States the week after next and there'll be a tremendous backlog of work. I can't let him down.'

'We must organise,' Jake said decisively, stretching out his long legs and lacing his fingers with hers.

'You're putting on your executive face,' she teased.

'Someone has to use a little sense, my beautiful girl. Now then, let's see.' His expression was thoughtful. 'You fly home, give in your resignation, buy your trousseau, find us a house close to London, locate a school for Benjy, and arrange our wedding.'

'All that?' Leigh gasped. 'How much time do I have?'

'A month. That'll give me time to finish off here and have my belongings shipped home. I'm sure my aunt will look after Benjy while we're on our honeymoon.'

'You appear to have everything organised already, Tuan Number One,' she grinned. 'I'm very impressed.'

'It's amazing what can be achieved with the right motivation,' said Jake, making a grab for her. He was in the process of kissing her thoroughly when the familiar toot of Frank's horn broke his concentration. As Jake opened the front door Leigh dragged a comb through her hair. Her head swam when she stood up, but she was too happy to decide whether it was from the effect of the brandy, or Jake, or both. She picked up her totebag and went outside to the porch to greet Frank.

'How are you, young lady?' he enquired, casting a critical eye over her. 'You look as though you've had a hectic time. I should think you're ready for bed.'

Jake grinned at her delightedly.

'It's been a busy day for you,' Frank continued, oblivious of the shared intimacy of their look. 'What with rescuing Benjy and nearly getting drowned. How is the little lad?'

'He's fine,' Jake responded, a smile still lurking in the corner of his mouth. 'He hardly woke up at all when we put him to bed. I expect he'll be bouncing around as usual first thing in the morning.'

'That's good news. Come along, Leigh, Bridget'll be anxious to hear what's happened.'

'I bet she will,' Jake remarked drily. Frank walked around the car and sat down in the driver's seat, fumbling to fill his pipe from a tin of tobacco he had produced from the dashboard compartment.

Jake caught hold of Leigh's arm as she made to follow her host. 'Kiss me goodnight,' he ordered with mock severity.

'Again?' She raised her brows in laughter.

'Again, and again, and again,' he whispered, closing his arms possessively around her, his mouth tasting hers in sweet sensuality. 'Don't say anything to Bridget,' he said mischievously. 'Just tell her you'd like me to come to dinner tomorrow evening. It'll be interesting to see her reaction when we tell her we're going to be married. I bet you a million dollars she'll take all the credit.'

'Despite the fact that she nearly ruined everything with her innuendoes!'

Jake laughed. 'But to her eternal credit she did set up the Hong Kong connection.'

'Very pretty,' said Bridget, standing back and surveying the table. 'That idea of yours to place an orchid at each setting makes the table look very elegant.'

Leigh's mouth twisted into laughter, the pale purple orchids were a touch she knew Jake would appreciate.

'I'm so glad you've cheered up,' said Bridget, smoothing down the skirt of her bright turquoise hostess gown. 'That touch of sea air must have done you a power of good, you've hardly stopped smiling all day.'

Leigh made a noncommittal gesture as she followed her hostess back into the kitchen.

'All prepared,' the older woman ticked off the menu on her fingers. 'Smoked salmon, followed by fillet steak, and fresh fruit salad for dessert.'

'A meal fit for a king.'

'Fit for a Chairman,' Bridget retorted happily.

Leigh gave her an affectionate glance. Bridget's heart was in the right place, even if her love of gossip had proved rather troublesome. She twisted the silver bracelet at her wrist. Compared to Bridget's colourful outfit, she was extremely subdued, in a creamy jump-suit with a flowing overdress, caught at the waist with a silver clasp. Even the filigree drops in her ears paled to insignificance beside Bridget's huge emeralds.

Jake arrived bearing a huge sheaf of carnations which he presented to Bridget with great ceremony, while she blushed and twittered like a schoolgirl. His blue eyes sought Leigh's over her hostess's bright head and he smiled, drawing her into a look of love that needed no further confirmation. He looked debonair and virile, in a dark suit and snow-white shirt, and Leigh's heart skipped a beat as he walked over to pull her close and kiss her deeply. Bridget watched speculatively as Jake sat down on the sofa close to Leigh and calmly accepted the gin and tonic Frank offered. When everyone was sipping their drinks he looked across at Bridget with a level serious gaze.

'Isn't it about time you owned up?' he asked, laughter pulling at the corner of his mouth.

'Owned up to what?' she asked, puzzled.

'To interfering in other people's lives.'

'Oh, I didn't!' she declared hotly, the colour rising in her cheeks.

Jake placed a possessive arm around Leigh's shoulder. 'You *didn't*!' he repeated, arching a brow. 'What about your performance with Leigh and me? You fixed up the Hong Kong trip, didn't you?'

'Not really . . .' She fingered an ear-ring. 'Well, perhaps.'

'Own up,' Jake chided. 'And you arranged our day out yesterday.'

'I never did,' Bridget said defiantly. She looked across at Frank, who gave a laugh.

'I did that,' he admitted.

Jake and Leigh looked at each other in surprise. 'You?' they echoed in unison.

Frank puffed contentedly at his pipe. 'It was obvious the two of you were in difficulties, so I decided to play Cupid.'

'Good grief!' Jake expostulated. 'Everyone was in on the act!'

'It worked, though,' Frank said smugly.

Bridget rounded on him. 'What do you mean?' she asked indignantly.

'He means that Leigh and I are going to be married,' Jake grinned.

Her lipsticked mouth fell open, and everyone laughed. She gave a swoop of delight, hugging and kissing them both in turn. 'I always knew it,' she declared. 'You two are made for each other.'

'Oh yes?' Jake commented drily. 'Then how do you explain your efforts to promote Rory?'

'Rory's just a boy,' Bridget declared dismissively.

'He's old enough to be a father,' Jake told her. 'He's taking Choo and their son to live in Bali.' Bridget's eyes opened wide. 'But that is classified information,' Jake said firmly. 'Not to be repeated, understand?'

'Yes, Jake,' Bridget agreed meekly.

Frank rose from his chair. 'We must celebrate. I've been saving up a special magnum of Krug champagne, and I reckon tonight's the night to open it.' He hurried off towards the kitchen, his face aglow with pleasure.

Jake squeezed Leigh's hand and gave her a sly wink. 'If I were you, Bridget, I'd keep an eye out for boyo there.' He jerked his head at Frank's retreating back. 'Rumour has it there are an awful lot of young ladies walking around with ash down their cleavages.'

'Oh, you!' Bridget gave him a playful push.

'Perhaps Frank's fancying a second time around,' he said, his eyes on Leigh. 'They say it's a littler lovelier, and believe me, it is.'

Harlequin® Plus

SOLE VERONIQUE

When Jake takes Leigh out to dinner in Hong Kong, they skip Chinese fare and opt instead for European food. Leigh selects a popular classic French dish—Sole Véronique, served with wild rice and *courgettes* (French for zucchini). You can easily prepare your own Sole Véronique at home by following these easy directions:

What you need:

¼ tsp. salt	1 lb. sole fillets
fresh-ground pepper to taste	2 tbsp. butter
¼ tsp. nutmeg	1 cup seedless
¼ cup all-purpose flour	green grapes
½ cup milk	⅓ cup whipping cream

What to do:

Combine salt, pepper, nutmeg and flour on a plate. Dip fish fillets in milk, then press onto flour mixture until thoroughly coated. Shake off excess. Melt butter in large, medium-hot frying pan, add fish and cook approximately 3-4 minutes on each side (fish is done if thickest part flakes when prodded with fork). Place fish in serving dish or on individual plates, and keep warm. Turn frying pan to high heat and add grapes. Stir quickly till warm, then spoon over fish. Add cream to hot skillet and bring to a boil, stirring constantly till cream turns a golden color. Pour over fish and grapes and serve at once. Serves 4.